Pride Publishing books by Thom Collins

Single Books
Closer by Morning
Silent Voices

Anthem
Anthem of the Sea
Anthem of the Dark
Anthem of Survival

Success
Never Too Famous

Jagged Shores
North Point

Anthologies
Brothers in Arms: Gods of Vengeance
Right Here, Right Now: The Coach

Jagged Shores

NORTH POINT

THOM COLLINS

North Point
ISBN # 978-1-83943-900-1
©Copyright Thom Collins 2020
Cover Art by Louisa Maggio ©Copyright July 2020
Interior text design by Claire Siemaszkiewicz
Pride Publishing

Published in 2020 by Pride Publishing, United Kingdom.

Pride Publishing is an imprint of Totally Entwined Group Limited.

NORTH POINT

Dedication

To the brave volunteers of the Royal National Lifeboat Institution. Every one of them a hero.

Chapter One

It was early evening in mid-July. A strong breeze came in from the east as Arnie Walker and AJ, his nine-year-old son, reached the top of the point. The sky was an unspoiled blue, but the wind whipped around them, pulling at their hair and clothes, and Arnie was glad he'd made the boy put on a hoodie before leaving their holiday home.

"You're not cold, are you?"

"No way," AJ replied, hurrying ahead.

"Stay away from the edge," Arnie warned.

North Point stood a hundred and six feet above the town of Nyemouth on the Northumberland coast, where the River Nye met the North Sea. From its peak they could see the entire town beneath them, nestled in the steep valley. The river ran through the center of the gorge, a broad curving waterway separating the two sides of the town. On the south bank, in a wide basin, was the marina, and just beyond, the green park and bandstand in the town square.

Ahead of them, to the east, was the vast, open vista of the North Sea. The strengthening wind created white tips on the waves of the incoming tide. Arnie gazed appreciatively at the view, filling his lungs with fresh, salty air. He'd missed this place. Coming here now, with his son, awoke memories of his own childhood, long-ago summers when he'd played on the point and the beach below, fishing in the rock pools at low tide or watching the yachts sail into the harbor. Some of the happiest, most innocent days of his life had been spent here.

"Dad, can we go down to the beach?" AJ asked.

Arnie saw some of that long-lost innocence in his son's face. He heard it in the pitch of his voice. "Not tonight. The tide is coming in. Besides, we'll be having dinner soon. Aren't you hungry?"

AJ stared at the rocks below and the sandy stretch of beach farther north. "The sea is miles out yet. Can't we go down for ten minutes? Five?"

"I'll take you to the beach tomorrow. I promise. The tide might look a long way out now, but it comes in fast. Really fast. The path to get down is a good mile ahead. By the time we get there, that beach will be gone. And we don't want to get stuck down on the rocks. The sea can come in and wash you away. It's dangerous."

AJ gazed longingly at the shore, unconvinced by his father's warning.

"Tomorrow," Arnie said firmly. "Remember, we've a whole five weeks ahead of us. That's plenty of time to play on the beach. When the summer is over, you'll be sick of picking sand out of your bum."

AJ giggled, thumping his hand playfully against his father's waist. "Sand doesn't get in your bum."

"Sand gets *everywhere*. In between your toes, in your ears, in your hair." He mussed AJ's short blond hair for effect.

The boy squealed with delight and squirmed away. "Stop it."

"Come on, we'll walk five more minutes before heading back. Are you hungry yet?"

"No."

"Well, I'm starving, so let's go."

They continued north along the cliff, keeping clear of the edge. Safety on the point had been something drilled into Arnie by his own parents from a young age, and it was a message he'd never forgotten. Like all coastal areas, the cliffs and rock faces here suffered from erosion and collapses. Harsh winters and rough seas took their toll.

When Arnie was AJ's age, the father of a boy from school had been killed on a beach outside of town when the cliff face collapsed. It was a vivid memory. Another summer, two people had died when they'd fallen over the edge and had been washed out to sea. A week later, one of the bodies had become tangled in the nets of a fishing boat. They had never recovered the second corpse. Despite the beauty here, there was immense danger. The natural elements had to be respected at all times.

Arnie had spent his life until the age of eighteen in Nyemouth, in the town below. He had moved to London to study drama and film editing but had never lost touch with the area. His parents were still here, in the house he grew up in. Though his career prevented him from coming back as often as he'd like to, a part of his heart remained.

Arnie Walker was thirty-four years old. He had dark blond hair, thick on top and conservatively short at the back and sides. His eyes were an intense, icy shade of blue. With an angular jaw and wide mouth, he was classically handsome. His six-foot-four frame and wholesome good looks were a striking combination. Arnie was a familiar one to TV audiences, having starred in several high-profile series, but despite a brief period of international success in his midtwenties, he could walk around without attracting too much attention. He'd never been the type to court publicity, avoiding the media throughout his career and preferring to focus on his work. Though they recognized him, most people respected his privacy, especially when he was with AJ.

That was especially true here in Nyemouth. It was a small community with a population of just over six thousand. Many of the long-time residents knew his family or remembered him as a kid. Arnie Walker was just a local boy who'd done well for himself. He'd never lost touch with where he came from. A Nyemouth boy, he was one of them, and people respected him for that.

"Dad, can we get a dog?"

An inevitable question, though Arnie hadn't expected to hear it so soon. They'd arrived yesterday and had spent two days catching up with family, including his sister and her black Labrador, Benji. AJ had fallen in love with the animal at first sight.

"We don't have time to look after a dog properly," Arnie said.

"We can make time."

"It's not that easy. I have to go to work. You have to go to school."

"I'll look after it. I'll get up extra early to take it for walks."

"And what will it do all day when we're not there? Dogs need to go out for the toilet. It's not fair to leave them locked up so long."

"It can stay in the garden when we're out."

"And in the winter? When it gets cold. Then what?"

"You can buy him a kennel."

Typical kid, Arnie thought. He had an answer for everything. He'd been exactly the same at that age. It had probably driven his parents crazy. "Let's see how the summer goes," he said. "You can play with Aunty Sophie's dog and take him for walks."

"Then we'll get our own dog when we go home?" AJ's eyes were wide and opportunistic.

"I didn't say that."

"But you'll think about it?"

"We'll see how it goes. That's all I'll say for now."

AJ grinned, on the face of it convinced his father had committed to buying him a puppy. "Can we have fish and chips for dinner tonight?"

Arnie laughed. "If that's what you want."

A female runner came up behind them, swerved out of their way and jogged ahead, an impressive sight in her pale blue sportswear. Arnie watched her admiringly. He'd promised himself a couple of lazy days off before getting back into a fitness routine. The cliffs along the point would make an attractive route as long as the weather held. If he came out of town, followed the walking trail, then looped back around, he would arrive where he'd started on the north bank of the river. It would be a five-, maybe six-mile trek. Not bad at all.

"I think we'll turn around in another minute," he told AJ. The wind was strengthening and the warmth of the sun had faded in the early evening.

"Can we go for fish and chips, then?"

Arnie nodded. "I said so, didn't I? Am I right in thinking you're hungry now?"

"Starving," AJ said.

Up ahead, the runner drew level with a small, bushy hollow. As she passed, a figure stepped out of the bushes. Dressed in a black hoodie and dark pants, they must have been hiding there. In an instant, Arnie knew something was not right.

The dark stranger rushed at the woman, came up behind her and threw both arms around her. The next moment, the figure lifted her off her feet and carried her toward the cliff edge.

"Oh my God." Arnie couldn't believe what was happening. They were around two hundred yards ahead of them. "Stay here," he shouted at AJ, running forward.

The woman struggled in the stranger's grip, but he held her tight. She kicked her legs helplessly against empty air and the sound of her scream was carried away on the wind. It seemed to happen with the heavy feel of a nightmare. Arnie's legs were leaden as he ran toward them, making painfully slow progress. *This can't be happening.*

The stranger was less than two feet away from the edge of the cliff. They swung the woman to one side, gaining momentum, and as they did, Arnie caught a glimpse beneath the hoodie. Their features were black and blank—a ski-mask or balaclava under the hood. The stranger bent at the knees, then swung, straightened up and threw the woman clear over the edge.

With a roar of despair, Arnie pressed forward.

The woman appeared to hang weightless in the air — a terrifying trick of the mind — before she plummeted from sight. The hooded figure didn't wait to admire their malicious handiwork. They were already running back in the direction they'd come from. Arnie raced for the spot where he'd last seen the woman.

Please let her be hanging on, just over the edge. He knew before he got there it was a hopeless thought.

"Dad," AJ yelled from somewhere behind.

He was about to tell him to stay back when he remembered the danger they were in. He looked around. No sign of the stranger, but it didn't mean the psycho had gone. Given the ease with which they'd thrown a grown woman over the cliff, a boy like AJ would take no effort. "Come here," he urged. "Stay close."

"What happened to the lady?" AJ asked.

"That's what Daddy needs to find out." Arnie glanced around again. The hollow from where the stranger had ambushed the woman was clear. There was no one else in sight. He pointed at the area. "AJ, I want you to keep looking that way. Do you hear me? Keep watching in that direction and if you see anyone coming — anyone — you shout at the top of your voice. Do you understand?"

Pale-faced and shaken, AJ nodded.

"Good lad," Arnie said, managing to sound far calmer than he felt. "Dad is going to see if he can help the lady, but remember, I want you to shout as loud as possible and let me know if anyone comes this way."

He nodded vigorously. "I will."

Arnie took a deep breath and approached the precipice. The grassy surface gave way to sandstone for the last few feet. Craning forward, he looked down. The tide came across the rocks below with some force, throwing up huge white plumes. He couldn't see her.

"Hello," he yelled, holding out hope she was clinging to the rock face below him. "Can you hear me?"

Nothing, just the crash of waves and the howl of wind. He put his foot right on the edge and leaned farther out. Now he could see more of the base. There she was. A tiny figure, a hundred and fifty feet below, in her blue and black Lycra. She lay face down, one arm beneath her, the other stretched to the side, about two meters from where the waves crashed against the rocks.

"Shit." It would not take long for the tide to reach her. He pulled his phone out of his pocket and dialed emergency.

"Which service do you require?" asked the operator.

"Coastguard," he said urgently. "A woman has gone over the cliff at North Point." He explained what had happened as calmly as he could and gave their exact position. "She's beneath me right now, but hurry. The tide is rising fast. She doesn't have long."

There was a lifeboat station in Nyemouth marina. Once a crew was assembled, it would only take the boat minutes to reach this spot, but raising a crew was a bigger concern. Like most lifeboat stations, Nyemouth was run by volunteers. Their pagers would already have gone off, but the boat, an Atlantic 85, required a crew of at least three before setting off. Depending on where they were when the pagers sounded, it could take ten minutes before the boat was ready to launch.

Looking at the incoming tide, Arnie wondered if the woman had that long. There was no way to reach her from here. The rock face was steep . A proficient climber with the right equipment could do it, but they would never get the woman back up that way. The only other route was the distant footpath down to the beach, but the section of rocks on which she lay would already be cut off by the tide.

The lifeboat was her only hope of survival. Provided they reached her in time.

Provided she was still alive.

"Dad," AJ called from behind. "Dad, is the lady okay?"

The boy was facing the other way. Arnie went to him. He trembled, frightened and cold. Arnie crouched and put his arms around him. "Don't worry. The lifeboat will soon be here. They'll look after her."

"Why did the man throw her off the cliff?"

He hugged AJ tighter. "I don't know, son. Try not to think about that. The man has gone now."

"He…he might come back."

"Sssh. It's all right. I won't let him hurt you."

They had witnessed a murder. An attempted murder at best. *Impossible.* It was what happened in TV shows and movies. In his own career, Arnie had played victims and murderers, but it was always fake. Even with detailed research, he'd never considered the reality of the crime. Until now. Watching a man — surely it had to be a man — pick up a woman and throw her over a huge precipice without hesitation.

A cold shudder ran through him.

It was an act of complete evil. Would AJ ever be the same after seeing that?

Arnie rose, stretching to look down into the Nye valley. Too far away to make out any activity in the marina. How long had it been since he'd made the call? Five minutes? Longer? Then he saw it. The gray and orange streak as the Atlantic 85 lifeboat shot out of the marina, leaving a wide wake as she headed for the mouth of the river and the open sea. *Thank God.*

Arnie told AJ to stay where he was while he went to look down again. The sea was lapping over the edge of the rocks, the spray washing over her body. His heart raced faster. She did not have long until the cold water claimed her. The lifeboat had turned left out of the river mouth and powered up the coast.

Would they even see her? How visible could a prone figure at the foot of a cliff be to anyone watching from the sea? He looked down again. She was so tiny. They'd be sure to miss her.

Arnie pulled out his phone and activated the flashlight. He was directly above the woman. He stood with the phone held high, the light directed toward the boat.

"Come on," he cried, desperately. "She's here. Right here."

"Dad," AJ called. "Is the lifeboat coming?"

It did not look like it. The boat cruised north, scanning the shore. They were going too far. Arnie stretched higher, waving his phone frantically.

"Over here." AJ, right behind him, waved his arms and shouted. "Here."

"Don't come too close," Arnie warned him.

"But they're going the wrong way."

Then, at sea, the boat turned and headed directly toward them.

"They've seen us," he told AJ with relief. "It's all right, they've seen us."

They fixed the boat on the spot where the woman lay. With the treacherous rocks and back flow from the waves, getting to her would not be easy. The Atlantic 85 was built for maneuverability, but even that would struggle in these circumstances.

Arnie prayed they were not too late.

Chapter Two

Dusk was cutting in when Arnie and AJ reached the marina. They had watched the difficult rescue operation from the cliff top. It had taken numerous attempts to back the boat close enough to the rocks to allow two members of the crew ashore to tend to the victim. From what he could see, the woman remained unconscious throughout as the team carefully transferred her to a spinal board then onto the craft. The great care taken by the rescuers told Arnie one important thing — she was still alive.

The crew were dealing with a casualty, not a body. The realization gave him some relief.

An ambulance was parked outside the lifeboat station with its blue lights flashing. They had already taken the victim on board by the time they got there.

Arnie's parents were waiting on the waterfront. His mother wrapped her arms around him and AJ as soon as they appeared.

"My God, this is awful," she said, kissing Arnie on the cheek before attending to his son.

Elizabeth and Martin Walker had been active supporters of the Nyemouth lifeboat station since before Arnie was born. Elizabeth had been the chairperson of the fundraising team for almost twenty years.

"Are you boys okay?" his father asked, putting a hand on his shoulder. Martin Walker was fifty-nine with a full head of gray hair and pale blue eyes. Arnie had spent his entire time growing up being told by the people in town he looked just like his dad.

"We're fine," Arnie assured him. "Just a little cold, that's all. Mam, could you do me a big favor? AJ hasn't eaten. Would you take him to the fish and chip shop to get him some food?"

"Absolutely," she said, taking AJ's hand. "What about you? Want me to bring something back?"

"I'm fine for now," he convinced her. "If you could just take care of AJ, it would be a big help."

"Come on inside," his father said. "We'll get you warmed up."

"How is the woman?" he asked as a paramedic shut the back doors of the ambulance and hurried around to the driver's side.

"Alive," Martin said. "Thanks to you. If you hadn't reacted as quickly as you did, I dread to think where she'd be. Come on, I want to get you a hot drink. You're trembling. Pale too. It's delayed shock. We need to get you warm."

Arnie allowed his father to lead him through the station to the crew room. Martin gave Arnie his jacket to put on top of his light summer hoodie and filled the kettle.

As the water boiled, the door opened and a thickset man in his late thirties entered. He wore a black T-shirt and jeans. His dark hair was wet, and his broad face appeared flushed around the cheeks and brow.

Martin introduced them. "This is Dominic. He's helmsman on the crew that went out tonight. Dominic, this is my son, Arnie. He raised the shout."

Dominic offered his hand and Arnie accepted it gratefully. His grip was strong, the skin rough. His forearms bulged with muscle as they shook. "Good call," Dominic said. There was a tired look in his eyes. The adrenaline of the rescue would be wearing off. "We got there just in time. If we hadn't spotted your light, we might not have found her at all. That was a good idea of yours."

"How is she?"

"Not good. There were some broken bones, that much was obvious, but it's the injuries that can't be seen I always worry about. We had to suspect spinal damage and use utmost caution."

"Shit. That poor woman."

"Is it true what they're saying out there?" Dominic asked, his dark eyes looking directly at Arnie. "Someone threw her off the cliff?"

He nodded. "Unbelievable, isn't it? I saw it happened and I'm still struggling to believe it."

Dominic winced. "We all are."

Martin put a mug of tea and a plate of biscuits in front of Arnie. "Eat those too. You need the sugar for the shock."

He made a second cup for Dominic.

"The police are outside," Dominic said. "They want statements from all of us." He had large and very expressive brown eyes. Within them, Arnie saw flecks of amber and gold. With his dark hair and muscular build, Dominic looked every inch a hero.

No, Arnie corrected himself. *This guy doesn't look like a hero. He is a hero. The entire crew are.*

It was more than the way he looked. There was an aura about Dominic, an undefined energy that made him incredibly attractive. Arnie had worked with some exceptionally good-looking men in his career, bona fide Hollywood heartthrobs, and none of them had Dominic's naturally sexy quality. Everything about him — his face, his hair, his build — appealed. He was a knockout.

Come on, Arnie thought, pulling himself up. *You've just witnessed a horrendous crime. A woman is fighting for her life this very minute and you've taken a fancy to the local hot guy. Get a grip.*

He dunked a biscuit into the tea and ate it. His father was right — the sugar seemed to have an instant effect and his senses became clearer.

"How rough were things out there?" Martin asked.

"The sea's getting up," Dominic answered. "The wind too. Another half hour and we might not have got in there. It wouldn't have mattered if we did. The tide would have taken her by then. It doesn't bear thinking about."

"You're amazing," Arnie said, and meant it. Dominic and the crew of volunteers had risked their lives for the safety of a complete stranger. They might all have died trying to rescue her.

"I just drove the boat," he said. "My colleagues — Joanne and Minty — they did the hard work. They transferred the woman from the rock to the boat and kept her stable the whole way back. That's no easy job in those swells."

"Does anyone know who she is?" Martin asked.

"Minty thought he recognized her from around town but couldn't be sure. It's for the police to find out now."

"It's hard to believe something like this could happen here in Nyemouth," Martin said. "Something so cruel. Who do you think did it? An ex-boyfriend?"

Martin and Dominic looked at Arnie expectantly.

"I've no idea," he said at last, avoiding the intense scrutiny of Dominic's eyes. "Whoever it was, they kept their face hidden. It could be anyone. And they came from behind. So, even if it was someone she knows, I doubt she'd have recognized them."

"Bastard," Dominic said. He had a slight accent Arnie couldn't place. Northern. Maybe Yorkshire. Nothing definite. The accent of someone who moved around a lot, losing all but a trace of their regional twang. A bit like his own.

It was hard not to look at him. He was stunning. That hair, the glossy sheen of his beard, the moody furrow between his eyebrows. *Wow.* Despite everything that had happened, Dominic aroused something in Arnie. It should have been the last thing on his mind, but Arnie couldn't stop the desire he felt for him. He imagined holding him and kissing that mouth, thinking about the body beneath those clothes.

Stop it.

Arnie finished his tea. "I should speak to the police. The sooner they know who they're looking for, the sooner they'll find him."

"Are you feeling better?" Martin asked.

"Much," he assured his father. "Thanks to you."

"Take care of yourself," Dominic said. "I wish we'd met under better circumstances. Hopefully I'll see you around some time."

Those eyes were mesmerizing. They drew Arnie in. "I hope so too. We're here all summer, so I'm sure I'll run into you again." As he tore his gaze away from Dominic's, he couldn't resist one last look to check out his hands, or rather his fingers. Empty. No rings there.

So? That doesn't tell you anything. And you really shouldn't be thinking about stuff like that. Not right now.

He headed outside. The lifeboat, sitting on its carriage, was in the center of the station. A couple of crew members were hosing off the salt with fresh water.

News of the attack had spread, and a crowd of curious onlookers had gathered at the marina. Arnie went up to the first police officer he saw and identified himself as the emergency caller.

The PC told him to wait and a few minutes later he was introduced to a middle-aged detective with chestnut hair and overpoweringly sweet perfume. Arnie repeated the full account of what he had seen on the cliff—how the masked stranger had appeared from the hollow to grab the victim and carry out their terrible mission.

It hit him for the first time that the attacker must have been lying in wait for a suitable target. And if the runner hadn't come past when she did, then what? Just suppose AJ hadn't been right by his side when they had passed. If the boy had run ahead or lagged behind. A few seconds was all it would have taken to snatch him and carry him to the edge. A nine-year-old boy would be a far easier target than a grown adult. *Could a person be that crazy?* He shook his head, barely able think about it.

"What do you remember about the attacker?" the detective asked.

"Not much. It was over so fast. I was too shocked to take in much of the detail."

"Anything you recall will be a huge help. Were they tall? Thickset? Skinny?"

"They were average height and build, I would say. Five-eight or nine." He concentrated and tried to visualize the moment. "A little taller than the jogger. Their clothes were dark. A hoodie and trousers, maybe jeans. And beneath the hood, they wore some kind of ski mask over their face. Whoever they were, they took no chances."

"Can you make a guess as to their sex or age?"

He shook his head. "My natural inclination is to say it was a man, but it could just as easily have been a well-built woman. I don't know. With surprise on their side, it could have been either. I'm sorry."

"Don't worry. And where did they go afterward?"

"Again, it was all so fast, I didn't see. They headed back in the direction they came from. Beyond that hollow, they could have gone anywhere. Toward the golf course and the car park, or up onto the moors, or back down to the town. My God, they really did have this all planned out."

* * * *

Arnie and AJ arrived at the holiday house after eleven. It had been a long evening. When he'd finished with the detective, he'd sat down with a uniformed officer who'd taken a full written statement. They wanted to speak to AJ too, but he managed to put them off until morning. It was unlikely AJ could tell them any more than he had, and he'd been through enough for one day.

Cliff House, their summer let, was a grade II listed building, situated on North Point, a little over a mile from where the attack had occurred. It had seemed so idyllic when they'd arrived yesterday. Now Arnie wasn't so sure.

He drove into the central courtyard, which offered privacy as it was surrounded on three sides by the buildings, and made sure the electric gates had closed behind them. He'd chosen the house because of its location. Private and remote, it was perfect for their needs.

Now that remoteness and its proximity to the crime made him notice its flaws.

Rubbish. The CCTV and security system were better than they had at home. He was being overly sensitive, that was all. No surprise after what had happened.

He unlocked the door and led AJ inside.

"Can I watch some YouTube before bed?" AJ asked hopefully.

"No chance. It's far too late. Get ready for bed. I'll be up in a minute."

Arnie walked through the ground floor, turning on lights and closing the curtains. During the day, the views from the house were spectacular from every aspect, but at night, there was nothing out there but darkness. Anyone could be hiding in the shadows.

Cliff House dated back to the 1890s but had undergone extensive interior renovations in the last decade. Modern and well-equipped, the inside skillfully blended the past and present with a state-of-the-art kitchen, heating and air-conditioning, together with real wood floors and a log-burning stove.

When they'd heard he would spend five weeks in Nyemouth, Arnie's parents had told him to stay with them, but he'd wanted his own space and independence. It was one thing to return to his hometown for the summer, but another to move back into the house they had raised him in.

AJ was in bed wearing Harry Potter pajamas when Arnie went up to his room.

"Did you wash your face and brush your teeth?" he asked.

"Yes."

"Prove it," Arnie said, leaning close. AJ breathed minty freshness over his face. "Good boy." He tucked the covers in around him.

"Dad, why do you think the man did that to the lady?" AJ's eyes were heavy as he fought exhaustion.

"I don't know, son, but try not to think about it now."

"What if he comes back? We're close to the cliff. He could push us over."

"We're locked in safe and secure. Nobody can get in the house, so you need not worry about that. Okay. Get some sleep." He kissed AJ on the forehead.

"Will you leave the bedroom door open? And the landing light on?"

"Sure. Now go to sleep and don't worry. Goodnight."

"Goodnight, Dad."

In the kitchen, Arnie took a bottle of Shiraz from the wine rack, opened it and poured himself a generous glass. The wine needed time to breathe, but after swirling it around the glass a couple of times, he drank. He needed it. He was hungry too. Besides the biscuits at the lifeboat station, he hadn't eaten since lunchtime. In the fridge, he found a pack of roasted chicken breasts and a tub of coleslaw. It was better than nothing and he was too weary to cook. He made a sandwich and devoured it at the breakfast bar.

Finished, he took the wine into the living room and dropped gratefully onto the soft, beige-colored sofa.

How quickly things had changed. Yesterday they'd been father and son at the start of their summer holidays, a whole adventure ahead of them. Now Arnie did not know what tomorrow would bring but suspected it would not be good.

They had come to Nyemouth to get away from London and escape the media attention they'd been under. When the press realized he'd played a small role in tonight's rescue, they would come calling. They would find out too—no doubt about that. There were few secrets in their lives right now.

Arnie had had full-time custody of AJ for the last five years, since his divorce. His marriage to Tara Westmoorland, a society girl and sometime model, had been a disaster. A closeted actor and a fame-hungry party girl—they'd been damned from the start.

Tara had seduced him at the London premiere of an action movie in which he'd played the secondary lead to a huge American star. Encouraged by a PR manager who had wanted to keep Arnie's sexuality under wraps for fear it would damage his burgeoning film career, and Tara, who had wanted to exploit their relationship for fame, he'd gone along with the charade. Being photographed and seen with Tara kept awkward questions about his sexuality at bay. When Tara had fallen pregnant a few months after they met, they'd arranged a hasty wedding.

Despite everything, Arnie was determined to be a good father, and when AJ had been born, he'd never been happier.

The marriage had been a disaster on an epic scale. They'd argued all the time and slept around. Arnie had had several male lovers while Tara had fallen back into her old party lifestyle of sex, drugs and alcohol. Her exploits, regularly stumbling out of nightclubs at four a.m., became a favorite for gossip columnists, and paparazzi followed her whenever she left the house.

They had divorced after four years.

Tara's behavior had become wilder in the aftermath. She didn't seem to care who she was seen with and what they were photographed doing. When she was pictured taking coke in a supermarket carpark with a four-year-old AJ in the back seat, it was front page news.

Arnie had been dividing his time between work in the UK and America. When the photos of Tara snorting cocaine off her acrylic nails while AJ played with action figures in the background hit the news, he'd canceled all his commitments in the USA and had returned to England to take care of his son full time. AJ was his top priority. Though he continued to work, he chose his roles based on location, ensuring he could stay home and give AJ the stability he needed.

He protected him from the attention of the press as much as he could, sheltering him. Until recently, that had not been difficult. The media had respected those boundaries.

Until Easter this year.

When Tara had gotten involved with Richie Hughes, a hard-drinking, hard-drugging rock star, she'd become front page news again. They were the out-of-control couple the press and public loved to hate. Overnight, Arnie noticed that he too had become a person of interest. Photographers lurked at the end of the street and inundated his agent with requests for interviews. Everyone wanted to know his opinion on his ex-wife's latest behavior. He turned them all down.

Three weeks ago, Tara and Richie had gotten married in Las Vegas. The wedding photos were everywhere. Both of them high, Richie wore scruffy jeans and a T-shirt, while Tara wore a barely there dress, slit to the waist front and back. An Elvis impersonator conducted the wedding.

Since then, press interest had rocketed. Arnie had known the best thing he could do was to get AJ away from London and the pack of journalists camped outside their house. Family, stability, normality — that was what they both needed.

A return to Nyemouth had seemed like the perfect solution.

No pressure. No stress. AJ could spend time with his grandparents and play with his cousins. He could enjoy the beaches and the landscape. An ideal summer.

The idyll had lasted exactly a day.

After what they had witnessed tonight, Arnie feared nothing would ever be the same again.

Chapter Three

Dominic Melton and Jacob Chisholm were the last to leave the lifeboat station. They locked up just before midnight. The police, having taken statements from all members of the crew involved in the rescue, had gone. So too had the onlookers. Most emergency shouts drew a small crowd of observers, the concerned and the curious, but Dominic couldn't remember seeing as many people as had come out tonight.

Their interest was no surprise. If what Arnie Walker and his son claimed to have seen were true, he'd never been on a shout quite like this either.

After securing the station, Dominic and Jacob headed along the front of the marina, to the stone steps that led to South Bank Terrace. Dominic's house, overlooking the bay, was less than five hundred yards from the lifeboat station. When his pager had gone off just before seven that evening, he'd run straight there. It was quicker than getting in the car and navigating the narrow back streets to the marina.

Jacob, the seventy-year-old treasurer of the Nyemouth lifeboat committee, was also Dominic's neighbor.

"How about a nightcap?" Jacob said as they reached the top of the steps and turned along the terrace toward their houses.

"Good idea, but I need to take the dog out first," Dominic said. "She's been shut in all evening. Ten minutes?"

"I'll have 'em ready," Jacob said, opening the gate at the bottom of his garden and heading up the path.

Dominic lived in the end house, a three-bedroom sandstone with exceptional views of the harbor and bay. The house, dating back to 1889, was one of the oldest in town, and although he'd only lived here for five years, the property gave him a deep connection to the area and its history.

Brandy, an eight-year-old mongrel, greeted him at the door with an enthusiastic tail wag.

"I know I'm late, girl," he said, crouching to rub the dog behind her ear. Brandy nutted him affectionately in the chest. Dominic had adopted her from a rescue center eighteen months earlier, when her previous owner, an elderly lady, had passed away. He'd never quite figured out the different breeds that made up her mix, but Alsatian was the most recognizable.

He grabbed the dog's leash, a torch, a roll of poo bags and his leather jacket before going back out into the night. The wind that had sprung up around five and made the rescue operation so difficult had increased, leading to an unseasonably cold evening. In the distance, he could hear the rough sea breaking on the beach. He hoped there would be no more emergency calls tonight.

He walked the dog up onto the headland and waited for her to do her business in one of her usual spots before cleaning up and turning for home.

Jacob had left his front door unlocked. He was waiting in the living room with a bottle of Haig Club, two lead crystal tumblers and a small jug of water.

"So, we're drinking the good stuff tonight," Dominic said, removing his jacket and taking the armchair next to Jacob while Brandy got comfortable at his feet.

"After a shout like that, I figured you deserve a shot of something decent. None of that own-brand firewater."

"You'll get no argument from me." Dominic added a drop of water to the glass of scotch and sipped. The smooth whiskey warmed his throat on its way down. He sighed appreciatively.

Jacob held his own glass in two hands and leaned deep into his chair. They'd been friends since the day Dominic moved to Nyemouth. The widower had knocked on his door as the last of the removal men departed. Within twenty minutes, they'd been sitting in the garden, gazing at the sea and bonding over a glass of scotch. The moment had defined their relationship ever since. Jacob had a thick sweep of white-gray hair and keen blue eyes. When he had welcomed Dominic to the town, he'd known right then that he would like it here.

"What do you make of all this business tonight?" Jacob asked. "Think it was a local fella, or just some random nutcase passing through? A psychopath who spotted an opportunity?"

"Some opportunity," he said. "I don't know. It sounds too bizarre to be a random attacker, don't you think? Maybe it was deliberate. An ex-boyfriend, or someone she turned down who decided to get his own back. Someone who knew where the woman went jogging and at what time."

"It's an extreme form of payback," Jacob said.

"People do extreme things when they're under pressure. Remember that guy. Terry, something or other. When was that? Two years ago?"

"Terry Sanders," Jacob said, swallowing his drink and reaching for a refill. "That was different. Terry was depressed."

Terry Sanders had been a regular summer visitor to Nyemouth with a static caravan on the site outside of town. When his wife of ten years had left him, taking their three children with her, he'd struggled to cope. People who knew him well said they didn't believe he intended to take his own life, that what he did was an attention-seeking cry for help. They said when Terry had leaped off the pier one Saturday afternoon in late August, he couldn't have known the strength of the currents. Witnesses reported that he had surfaced once before the sea had taken him for good. The lifeboat and Coastguard helicopter had searched for seven hours that night without success.

Terry's body had become tangled in fishing nets two days later.

"I just mean people do things that are completely out of character when they're stressed," Dominic said. "It's possible a jilted ex with a big chip on his shoulder could decide the best thing for their relationship is to shove his beloved off a cliff. Some fucked-up if-I-can't-have-you-nobody-can way of thinking."

"You might be right. In an awful way, it will be good if you are. The police will find out soon enough if there's an inadequate loser in her background and that will be that. They'll slap the cuffs on and bring him in. But if the woman wasn't targeted for personal reasons, if it was a random attack and she was in the wrong place at the wrong time, then it could happen again. The woman survived. Tonight's failure might make him more determined to succeed."

Dominic exhaled through his teeth. "It sounds far-fetched. Like a plot from a detective show."

Jacob's eyes glistened in the soft light. "Excuse me, but who rescued a woman with potential spinal injuries tonight? It wasn't me. That's not far-fetched. You did it. It's a fact."

"Point taken." He reached for the square-cut whiskey bottle, poured another measure, and added a dash of water. "I picked up a bottle of Ardmore today, if you'd like to call round through the week and help me drink it."

"You're on," Jacob smiled.

They sat in silence for a few minutes. It was a testament to their friendship that they could enjoy the quiet moments. A framed photo of Jacob's late wife, Annabelle, smiled at them from the wall above the mantelpiece. She had died the year before Dominic had come to town, but Jacob spoke of her with such love, and with her pictures all over the house, he felt as if he knew her well.

As he sipped the whiskey and allowed it to do its work, Dominic's mind turned to Arnie Walker. He'd known Martin and Elizabeth Walker almost as long as Jacob, but tonight had been his first encounter with their famous son. He'd heard of him all right. The name Arnie Walker was a big deal in Nyemouth. As its most well-known former resident, it would be. But oddly, no one he'd met had ever had a bad word to say about Arnie. There appeared to be no small-town jealousy or envy where he was concerned. In Dominic's experience, that was very unusual. There was always some kid of resentment when a local boy made good.

It didn't appear true in Arnie's case.

Maybe it was because of his parents and popularity in the town.

Dominic did not watch a lot of television and had had no idea who Arnie was before moving to Nyemouth. Celebrity culture meant nothing to him. If he wasn't outside enjoying the beach or the moors, he'd rather spend his time with a good book than a TV show. But after getting to know and admire Martin and Elizabeth, he'd become curious about their son and had searched for him online.

The photos he'd found aroused his interest. Arnie was so much like his father. Dominic imagined that was exactly what Martin would have looked like twenty to thirty years ago. Fair-haired and handsome with twinkly blue eyes.

Arnie had starred in a lot of television shows and a handful of movies. Jacob owned many of them on DVD and had loaned them to him. Though Arnie was easy on the eye, most of the films he'd made were not Dominic's thing. Romantic comedies and period dramas. Nice enough to look at, but Dominic found them a chore to get through.

One thing he had learned tonight — the TV didn't do justice to Arnie's looks. On screen he appeared blandly pretty, like any random actor in a million rom-coms. Cute, for sure, but instantly forgettable, just like the movies. In reality, Arnie was a knockout. Despite the peculiar circumstances of their meeting, he'd made a huge impact.

His height, for one. At five-eleven, Dominic seldom felt short, but Arnie towered over him. Strange, considering all he'd ever heard about celebrities was how tiny they were in real life. And his face — so damn handsome, with that wide mouth and strong nose. Just like his dad, only younger and sexier. But it was Arnie's eyes that had really grabbed him. They weren't just blue, they were glacial. Startling. He couldn't remember when a man had last made such a powerful first impression on him.

"Arnie Walker seems like a nice guy," he said.

"Haven't you met before?" Jacob asked.

He shook his head. "Tonight was the first time. A bit odd, under the circumstances. It can't have been easy on him. Seeing that happen, with his boy there too. He looked shaken but holding up well, considering."

"Arnie's a good guy. He always has been."

"You must have known him a long time?" Dominic knew he'd asked the question before, but the answer had been lost in a haze of late nights and alcohol.

"All his life," Jacob said proudly. "I was at his christening. I remember him as a baby in the cot."

Jacob and Annabelle hadn't been able to have children of their own. Dominic wondered if that was one of the reasons he remembered Arnie so fondly.

"What was he like? As a kid, I mean."

"Never any trouble that I recall. He used to hang around the station in the school holidays. Martin was in the crew back then. Arnie was always there, showing an interest. Helping at the summer fair. If he hadn't moved away and done so well for himself, I reckon he'd be a member of the crew now."

The idea of working alongside Arnie gave Dominic a sudden and unexpected thrill. He wondered why the actor had had such a powerful effect on him. He appreciated Arnie's good looks as much as anyone, but he'd never been a fool for a pretty face. The attraction went deeper than that, and yet he didn't understand how it could. They'd met each other for such a short time and barely said more than hello. There had been no time to form any serious emotional contact. And he was still thinking about him.

Was he just starstruck? Unlikely, given how little attention he'd paid to Arnie's career before now.

"When did he move away?" he asked.

Jacob looked thoughtful. "My memory isn't what it used to be. At a guess, I'd say when he was eighteen. University time. I remember him playing the lead in an amateur production of *Saturday Night Fever* at the town hall, but he'd have been younger then. Around sixteen. He seemed to get into the drama at secondary school. That's where he caught the acting bug. He'd still lend a hand at the lifeboat fair, collecting money around the marina or selling raffle tickets, but we saw a lot less of him once he had taken up drama. It was obvious he had real talent, even then. No one else in *Night Fever* came close to matching him. Martin used to wonder where all his natural ability had come from. Martin's a great guy but he can't carry a tune."

"His folks must have been supportive. To encourage him with the acting."

"Oh, they sure were," Jacob said. "No parents could have been prouder. I remember the fuss they made when he got his first TV role. He played a murder victim on a cop show. You know the kind of thing — a body on the mortuary slab and a couple of short flashback scenes to show how he died. He couldn't have been on screen for more than three minutes or so, but Elizabeth behaved like he was the star of the show. Rightly so, I might add. It didn't seem like much later when he started taking the lead roles."

"He always stayed connected to Nyemouth?"

"Absolutely. When Annabelle was alive, she kept a scrapbook of all his interviews. Newspapers and magazines, that kind of stuff. Arnie has always spoken fondly of where he came from. And when he was too busy to get back for the annual lifeboat fair, he'd send on some cracking prizes for the raffle. All sorts of stuff from his movies and TV shows. One prize was an all-expenses-paid trip to New York to visit him on the set of a movie he was making there. It's strange how you've never met him until now. How you could have missed each other for five years, I don't know. Arnie has never lost sight of the town he grew up in."

Interesting. Until he came to Nyemouth, Dominic had never felt a connection to anywhere. Born in Cyprus, when his father, an RAF officer, had been stationed there, he'd spent his early years on the move until the family had settled in Yorkshire so he and his two brothers would be able to go to school. He'd joined the Royal Marines at eighteen and spent the next fourteen years working all around the world. Nyemouth was the only place he'd ever been able to call home.

Despite the glamour and excitement a life in show business must entail, he felt a new admiration for Arnie, for maintaining a strong connection to his family and community. A small part of him was even jealous.

"What about the boy?" he asked. "Does he live with Arnie?"

Jacob looked at him curiously. "Don't you read the newspapers?"

"Only for the news." He laughed. "I'm not really up on celebrity gossip. You know that."

"Seems like Tara Westmoorland is all over them these days. I don't know how you can avoid it."

"She's his ex-wife? The mother of the boy?"

"That's right. Seems like Tara has got herself in a real pickle of late. She was never the one for Arnie. That was obvious from the start. No one expected their marriage to last as long as it did, least of all Martin and Elizabeth. I don't think I've seen two people so happy about the breakdown of their son's marriage as they were. Tara and Arnie were all wrong for each other."

Though his knowledge of celebrity affairs was lacking, there was one thing about Arnie he did know — he was one of the most famous LGBTQ actors in the country. It was a bigger surprise to learn he had a kid from a previous relationship than the news that the golden boy of rom-coms was gay in the first place. There was no reason it should be. People were complicated. He knew that better than anyone.

"When they first separated, Arnie and Tara had joint custody of AJ," Jacob continued. "Arnie was out of the country a lot and it seemed to suit them both for a while. Only Tara was a wild one and a young child got in the way of her party lifestyle. I don't know how much Arnie knew already, but there was a big scandal when she threw a wild birthday party for herself at home. Someone thought it was a good idea to photograph AJ, who was around four at the time, with a crack pipe in his hand."

"Jesus."

"Inevitably, the photos were sold to the press and were tabloid front page one Sunday. There were others too. Tara taking drugs in front of the boy, that kind of thing. Arnie went ballistic and flew straight back from America. He's had full-time custody of AJ ever since. As far as I'm aware, Tara has never tried to contest it. She's too busy running around with her jet-set friends. Look her up sometime. You'll find plenty of good reading."

Dominic laughed softly. "I'll pass. I hate all that shit. Self-centered people with more money than sense."

"Tara maybe. Definitely not Arnie."

"No," Dominic said, thinking again about that handsome face and those incredible eyes. "He seems…nice."

"Nice?" Jacob said, shifting his gaze to meet Dominic's. "Do I detect more than casual interest?"

"Maybe." Then he shook his head. "No. No, I'm not interested in anything more," he said. An outright lie.

"Why not? Arnie is single at the moment. I'm sure of it."

"Really?"

"As far as I'm aware. If he's seeing anyone, he hasn't told his mother, 'cause she tells us everything." He laughed and sipped his drink. "I thought you were seeing Gabriel Mayne."

"Not really. We've…seen each other a couple of times. It's nothing."

"Well, then. You've got nothing to lose. Why don't you ask Arnie out? He's perfect for you. You'll be great together."

Dominic finished his drink. He'd had enough. It was time to go to bed. "I just…no. I'm not interested in a relationship with anyone. Arnie is a famous actor with a complicated lifestyle. That kind of bullshit is not for me."

The words sounded convincing. When waking up tomorrow, he hoped to believe them himself.

Chapter Four

After a restless night in which he couldn't have slept for more than a couple of hours, Arnie got up at six thirty and put on running shorts, T-shirt and sneakers. He looked in on AJ, still fast asleep with the covers pulled up to his ears, and went downstairs. Leaving the door open so he'd hear AJ if he woke, he went into the courtyard and performed a basic workout in the small open space. It was a standard boot camp routine of stretches, lunges, push-ups, burpees, star-jumps and a jog, around and around the yard. After half an hour his heart was racing and he'd built up a decent sweat.

It had been his intention to go for a long run on North Point today. After last night, he couldn't see that ever being a possibility. He would look into joining a local gym later in the week. It was a shame when there was such great countryside and so many beaches to get active upon, but from now on he would think carefully about where he went, especially with AJ.

It was a beautiful morning. The wind had died overnight and the sky was pure blue, promising a glorious day ahead.

Arnie went inside and poured a glass of cold orange juice. He grabbed his phone and checked for news on the state of last night's assault victim. There was a small feature on the regional North East page of the BBC website. The details were scant — a woman rescued by Nyemouth lifeboat after falling off the cliff. The unnamed victim was in a stable condition in hospital.

Arnie exhaled. *Thank God for that.* Stable didn't mean she was out of trouble. She could have all kinds of life-changing injuries, but she was alive. Not dead on the rocks or washed thirty miles out to sea. She had made it through the night. He would try to learn more about her later. Maybe visit her in hospital if that were possible. For now, he'd be grateful for the fact that she had survived.

When he went upstairs, AJ remained fast asleep. *Good.* At least he'd had a decent night. The police would come around at some point today, looking to get his side of the story. The little guy would have to go through it all again. For now, he could sleep.

Arnie dumped his clothes in the laundry basket and showered. After a rough night, it was amazing how much better a hard workout and a good wash made him feel. He stood beneath the faucet for a long time, allowing the hot spray to rain over his body. He tilted his head so the heat could get to work on the tension in his neck and shoulders.

As well as reliving the attack repeatedly throughout the night, he'd spent a good deal of time dreaming about Dominic. The crewman had made a strong and lasting impression in the brief time they'd shared. Little wonder, when he looked the way he did. Thickset and muscular, with that dark hair and those dreamy eyes, and the stubble on his broad chin so thick it was almost a beard. Thinking about him now made Arnie's pulse race.

He was a hell of a man.

How long had it been since he'd last had a guy? Arnie struggled to remember. There was Nick, a West End theater manager. They'd had a casual thing going, on and off for two years, after Arnie had appeared in a play there. It had never been serious. Arnie valued discretion and as Nick was also in the industry, he understood. He was a nice guy, good-looking and friendly, but it was nothing more than sex. Besides, Nick had started a new relationship, so they hadn't seen each other in, what, four months?

And before that? A fling last year with his costar on a low-budget British thriller. The man was as deeply in the closet as Arnie had once been, and there was no chance of it going further. The affair had been as brief as the three-week film shoot.

No wonder he'd taken notice of a hot guy like Dominic.

He was on the verge of becoming celibate.

He formed a mental picture of Dominic, trying to recall him exactly. Their meeting had been short. How much could he remember?

The dark hair and smoldering eyes for sure. Arnie had always had a thing for dark men. And meaty. *Oh, yes.* Dominic's broad, muscular build was exactly what he liked. It didn't matter that he was a good four to five inches shorter than Arnie. He was six-foot-four, and most guys were. Dominic was so rugged and masculine that the height difference did not matter.

He'd been wearing a black T-shirt and jeans. The way his clothes had clung to him hinted at a fine body beneath. The wide swell of his chest. The compact thickness of his waist. Arnie could easily imagine him naked, with solid thighs and a big, beefy butt. He hoped he was hairy too, that his muscular chest was covered in a luxurious spread of dark hair.

As he thought about Dominic naked, the effect was profound. Arnie caressed the full length of his hard cock and tugged his balls, imaging that powerful body next to his.

No. He caught himself. There was no time for this today. He turned the shower lever to cold and the icy water dwindled his erection in seconds. Thoughts of Dominic would have to wait.

Thoroughly dried, he checked his reflection in the mirror. He'd shaved on Saturday. Today was Monday. He ran his fingers over the bristles on his chin.

Fuck it!

Another day wouldn't hurt. He was on holiday. If he couldn't cut loose for a couple of days now, he never would. He washed his face and rubbed in a moisturizer with a basic 15 SPF. He towel-dried his dirty blond hair and texturized it with a tiny amount of wax.

It was seven thirty. Dressed in a pair of cream chino shorts and a navy linen shirt, he looked in on AJ. The boy lifted a sleepy head from the pillow.

"Morning, sunshine," Arnie said, sitting on the end of the bed. "Did you sleep well?"

AJ nodded, stretching beneath the covers and rubbing his eyes.

"Ready for some breakfast?" Arnie asked.

Another nod. AJ's hair stuck up at crazy angles.

Arnie patted his foot through the bed clothes. "Ten minutes, okay?"

In the kitchen, he put the kettle on to boil and set two places at the breakfast bar. There were fresh eggs in the fridge. *Poached eggs on toast. Perfect.* It would make a change from the cereal they'd had yesterday.

Arnie was still getting used to the layout of the kitchen and had to hunt through several of the cupboards to find a suitable pan. As he filled it with water, the intercom gave a loud buzz.

There was someone at the main gate.

Don't be the police, he thought. *Not this early.* He wanted AJ to have breakfast before giving his statement.

"Hello," he answered.

"Arnie Walker?" There was some distortion on the mic, but he didn't recognize the voice of the speaker.

"Who is this?"

A pause. "The name is Robert Goldman. I work for the *Northumberland Gazette*. I'm following up a story on the lifeboat rescue last night. I understand you were involved, Mr. Walker."

Shit. He should have known the press would get onto his contribution. There had been plenty of people at the station yesterday, and in a small town like Nyemouth, word got around fast.

"Mr. Walker," the reporter continued. "Is it true you made the emergency call to alert the Coastguard? Did you see the man who carried out the attack?"

"I've given a full statement on the matter to the police and have nothing further to add, other than that my thoughts and prayers are with the victim, and I wish her a speedy recovery."

"Can you confirm reports that a masked man threw the woman over the cliff?"

"I have nothing more to say and suggest you contact the local police for a statement." Arnie shut off the intercom.

Off the ground-floor hall was a small study where the CCTV controls were housed. He checked the camera on the front gate. He watched as a portly man in a badly fitting suit climbed into a white Nissan. So far it was only one reporter, and a local guy at that. It would be naïve to expect it to stay that way. The nationals would soon be onto it.

Tara and her rock-star lover, Richie, were in the gossip columns every other day. They were news. Though he did his best to avoid it, by default, it made Arnie and AJ newsworthy too.

He'd have to give them something to keep them off his case. They'd come to Nyemouth to escape media intrusion for the summer. That would all be ruined if the paparazzi came north and followed them around.

His only option was to make a statement. *And say what?* He knew nothing. He'd witnessed a crime and reported it. That was all he had to offer.

He would speak to the police first, so he didn't say anything stupid to the press that might harm their investigation.

* * * *

A police officer arrived just after ten. PC Romany. AJ was watching YouTube clips in the living room. Arnie took the officer to the kitchen.

"I hoped you could give me an update on the victim," he said.

"She's heavily sedated," PC Romany told him. "We haven't been able to speak to her yet, so it's vital we get all the information we can from witnesses such as yourself."

"I understand. Have you established her identity?"

She consulted her notebook. "Her name is Sandy Costello. Do you know her?"

"No. Sorry. I haven't heard of her. Does she live around here?"

"She does. On the Greenways Estate, on the south side of the river."

"It's awful. Does she have family here?"

"No. Ms. Costello lives alone. We're still trying to build a picture of her life. Her movements. Her friends. That kind of thing."

"You're not aware of any motive, then?"

"We're considering all lines of inquiry," she said with a tight smile.

"Of course."

Arnie sat with AJ while PC Romany took his statement. He answered all of his questions with a good recollection, even providing a clear description of the attacker's footwear, a detail Arnie had failed to notice. He was proud of him.

Afterward, he asked the officer for permission to post a brief statement on his social media account. He kept it vague, stating the fact that he had witnessed an incident and asking anyone with further information to contact the police directly. He said his thoughts were with the victim, without naming her, and that he hoped her assailant would be caught as quickly as possible. Romany read it back and gave her approval for him to post it.

Arnie hoped it would be enough to keep the press away, but he doubted it.

Later, he dropped AJ at his parents' house. They had offered to take him and his cousins to the cinema for the afternoon, figuring a movie would be a good distraction for the kids. Arnie thought it was a great idea and arranged to meet them later at a restaurant on the marina.

"Dinner's on me tonight," he'd said. "Don't be late."

With the afternoon ahead of him, he put on sunglasses and a hat and went for a walk. Generally, he could stroll around his hometown without being bothered, but given the circumstances and news coverage, he wanted to keep an even lower profile than usual. He'd had several missed calls from his agent. Listening to his voicemail confirmed the worst. He'd had a dozen requests for interviews from newspapers and TV shows that morning. Arnie called back and left a message with his agent's secretary.

"I won't be giving any interviews on this matter, so please turn down all requests," he said. "No exceptions. I'm off grid until the end of August. Please make sure it stays that way."

He'd committed to an independent movie that started shooting in London in late September. The filming dates fit perfectly with AJ's autumn term. After that, there was a TV show beginning in the new year. He had sufficient work to see him through the next nine months. That was good enough for now. He didn't want to be bothered with work-related calls when he'd set the summer aside to be with his son.

Arnie wandered through the town center. Nyemouth had altered little in the last thirty years. There'd been some major investment and regeneration of the harbor area, but the main square and shopping area were essentially the same as when he'd grown up here. A handful of businesses had changed ownership and there were more coffee shops than he remembered, but nothing much had altered.

His wandering took him to the marina. He had known from the outset that it would. Bright sunlight sparkled on the blue waters of the bay. Most of the boats in the fishing fleet were out. During summer, the inshore boats would return sometime between six and seven, while the larger trawlers would stay out at sea for four or five days at a time, as long as the weather permitted.

It was Monday. There were less tourists around than at the weekend, but as it was school holiday time, there were a few families enjoying the warm afternoon. Arnie fondly remembered days exactly like this from his own childhood, when freedom seemed endless, stretching ahead of him. He'd hoped that by bringing AJ to Nyemouth, his son could experience one of those timeless and magical summers for himself. Last night's incident had torpedoed any realistic expectation of that.

Arnie passed in front of the recently regenerated waterfront, past the restaurants and craft shops, and the specialist food stores selling local fish and produce. People sat outside the many bars and pubs, enjoying the terraces, drinking in the sun. He kept moving, not wanting to be seen or recognized, and without consciously planning it, found himself on the approach to the lifeboat station.

And there was Dominic.

The wide front doors of the station were open. Dominic appeared to be giving instructions to a younger man, gesturing toward the lifeboat.

He wore a dark gray T-shirt and cargo shorts. The outfit hugged his broad physique, contouring the muscles of his chest and shoulders, and the mighty fine sweep of his big arse. His skin was deeply tanned, an obvious benefit of his outdoor pursuits. No tattoos that Arnie could see, and he was quietly pleased. So many guys were excessively inked these days, that it was refreshing to find a man who wasn't.

He liked the short cut of Dominic's hair and the way it graded into the brown skin on the back of his neck. Despite its thickness on top, there was something military-looking in its practical style. And it suited him. A lot.

A queer feeling came over Arnie as he watched Dominic. It was unusual for a stranger to affect him in this way, on a purely physical level, provoking an odd, nervous sensation. It reminded him of live performance. Those last few tension filled minutes before going on stage — a mix of fear, anticipation and excitement.

Pull yourself together. This is no opening night. He's just a nice, regular guy. Go over and say hello.

Arnie took a deep breath and approached the station with a confidence he did not feel.

"Hi," he said, sounding light, casual. Like speaking to Dominic was no big deal.

Dominic turned. His dark eyes settled on Arnie and, as recognition dawned, Arnie could swear he saw them sparkle. A huge grin spread across Dominic's face, quite disarming in contrast with his naturally moody countenance.

"Hey. How are you doing?"

He stuck out his hand. Was it Arnie's imagination, or was Dominic's grip firmer and more lingering than last night?

"I'm good, thanks. I didn't expect to see you here today."

"I call by the station most afternoons," he said. "There's always something to be done. Maintenance, cleaning, inventory. After a shout like yesterday, I like to double-check that all the supplies we used have been replenished. The first aid kit and stuff like that. This is Noel," he said, introducing the young man with him.

Noel was in his late teens, with dark red hair and a freckled complexion. He smiled self-consciously and didn't offer his hand. He lacked Dominic's confidence, but Arnie supposed most other men would.

"Hi. Nice to meet you," Arnie said.

The boy nodded awkwardly. Arnie didn't pursue it further. He noticed that with a lot of young people these days — so many of them were lacking in basic social skills. He was determined AJ wouldn't fall into that trap.

"Have you got time for a drink?" Dominic asked. "Tea? Coffee? Something cold? We were just about to take a break."

"I'd love one, thanks."

He followed Dominic to the crew room. Last night, probably due to the shock, he'd failed to notice how little the station had changed since he helped out here as a kid. There were large boards on all the walls, noting the dates and times of all the major rescues the lifeboat had been involved with, going all the way back to 1864.

"Wow," he said, as they passed into the kitchen. "All this stuff, the history of the place, it meant nothing to me when I was young. I barely took any notice of it, but it's remarkable. It really is."

"That's how I feel too," Dominic said, filling the kettle. "When I arrived here and joined the crew, I used to spend hours reading the information on those boards. It's fascinating. An honour too, to play a small part in all of this." His eyes fell on Arnie's and lingered just for a second, before his mouth turned into an uncertain smile and he looked away.

"I'd hardly call what you do small," Arnie said. "Risking your own life to save others. I don't think the general public appreciate that. Those tourists outside, enjoying their beers in the sun, they'll have no idea that if they get into trouble on the water the people who'll save their lives will be volunteers."

"Were you ever in the crew?"

"No. I was too young. I was eighteen when I left Nyemouth. I always meant to join though. Growing up, I used to dream about going out on rescues."

"You got that from your old man?"

"I guess I did. How about you? What got you involved in the lifeboat? You're not from around here, are you? Is that a trace of Yorkshire I detect in your accent? It's subtle, but it's there. Am I right?"

Dominic chuckled. "Guilty as charged. We moved around a lot when I was young, but spent more time in Yorkshire than anywhere else. I guess that's what stuck. But no, there are no prior connections with the lifeboat. I was in the Royal Marines for eight years, and then another six in the Special Boat Service."

Arnie's eyes widened. The physique, the incredible build, the selfless bravery. It all made sense. Dominic was a real-life superman.

"By the time I left the service, I had the sea in my veins. The lifeboat offered the perfect opportunity to indulge my love of boats and action. You know what it's like. We do a lot of practice drills and rescues. It fills a space my career left in me."

"What do you do for a living?" Arnie asked, intrigued.

"I'm a writer," Dominic said, getting two mugs from the cupboard. "Tea or coffee?"

"Tea, please, with a splash of milk. Skimmed if you have it."

"Just semi," he said, opening the fridge.

"That'll do fine. What do you write?"

"Have you ever heard of Jack Cole?" Dominic asked, dropping tea bags into the mugs and pouring water over.

Arnie considered the question. The name was indeed familiar. He'd seen it embossed on the front cover of paperbacks. He'd never read Jack Cole, but he was sure, yes, of course — his dad had a couple of his novels on his bookcase. "The thriller author?"

Dominic grinned. He set the mugs down on the table and sat facing Arnie. "Jack Cole is me."

Arnie stared. "You're kidding? Wow." Why hadn't his parents mentioned this? His mother was usually keen to share any old boring trivia about people he might have known at school and had long since forgotten. She'd inform him in great detail about children, marriages, divorces, drinking problems, job successes and failures but he couldn't recall her ever mentioning this.

The more he thought about it, the more he realized Jack Cole was a big deal. One of those best-selling thriller writers whose books were given prominent shelf space around Father's Day and Christmas. Those military action stories had never appealed to him, but he would surely have taken notice if he knew the author lived in Nyemouth and volunteered in the lifeboat.

And looks like the man of my dreams.

"So, Jack Cole is a pen name?" he asked. "Because of your military background?"

"That's one reason. I write fiction, not those true-life armed forces bio books, but I like to keep a clear distance between my writing and my personal life. I don't want to be a celebrity author. I don't want to be recognized."

"I understand," Arnie said. "I often wish I could do what I do without the public recognition."

"I'm happy staying out of it. I don't usually tell people who I am. At least not straight away. I don't know why I blurted it out to you. It's not my style."

"I'm glad you did. My dad has some of your books. Now I have something to read this summer."

Dominic put his elbows on the table. His forearms were thick, nicely tanned and coated with dark, silky hair. Arnie's gaze drifted to his hands. They were large with thick fingers. The backs of his hands were marred with small cuts and pale scars. The hands of a practical man used to manual work, rather than a writer. He imagined those hands moving over his body, across his chest and stomach, going lower, sliding into his underwear to take him in a firm grip.

Arnie forced his attention back to Dominic's face, but those deep bedroom eyes did little to dispel his arousal.

"Your dad told me you're here until September," Dominic said.

"That's right. Five weeks is all. Until AJ goes back to school."

"You must feel a strong connection to the town. I mean, you could have taken your son anywhere in the world for the summer."

"I love it here," Arnie said. "I'd love to spend even longer, but it's impossible to maintain an acting career this far north. All my opportunities are in London. But I wanted AJ to experience more of Nyemouth than a couple of weekends a year and a few days at Christmas. It's a long story, but it's important for us both to have some stability right now."

Dominic sipped his tea. "Last night can't have helped. How is AJ today?"

"He seems fine. He was amazing giving his statement to the police this morning. I swear he has a better recollection of it than I do."

Dominic laughed. "Kids are like that. Full of surprises."

Arnie was desperate to discover more about this sexy hero. He spotted an opening and took it. "Do you have kids?"

"Me?" He grinned. "No way. We get a lot of kids down here at the station. School trips, special projects, volunteers, that kind of thing. Noel, the lad outside, he's been helping out around here since he was fifteen or so. The lifeboat is a big draw for the young ones."

"I remember. I used to be one of them." Dominic's smile might be the sexiest part of him. Arnie couldn't take his eyes off his mouth. It was wide and mischievous. *And flirtatious?* Maybe. "You're not married then?" The question was out the instant it came to mind. He regretted it as soon as he asked.

Dominic seemed not to mind. "No. I'm not married. I live up on South Bank Terrace. Just me and my dog, Brandy."

Sexy and single. *But whose team does he play for?* Arnie blocked that question before he blurted it out like the last one. He had a good feeling about Dominic, and he was giving out the right vibes. Dominic was into him. Arnie was certain of it. And he was flirting for sure. How could he not be with a smile like that?

He definitely likes me. A little bit. Maybe.

Arnie dismissed the idea. So what if he did? Now was not the time to even entertain the idea. He was here for AJ, not to fall for the local action man. The boy's life was chaotic enough with his mother running around and getting high with her rock-star husband. Arnie had to be better than that.

Dominic might just be the sexiest, most charismatic man in Nyemouth, but Arnie had to stay immune to him.

Romance was not on the agenda this summer.

That was the way it had to be.

Chapter Five

Arnie arrived at The Lobster Pot before any of his family. His mother had sent a text to let him know they were on their way but stuck in traffic.

Aside from a handful of pubs, The Lobster Pot restaurant was one of the oldest joints in town. It had been run by the same family for all of his life. Like other properties on the waterfront, it had benefitted from the vast regeneration of the area. Despite the modern refit, the restaurant kept a first-rate reputation for serving some of the best seafood in the whole North East. It was a hard-earned status, built over decades, and customers traveled from around the UK to enjoy the menu.

Arnie realized it was probably a little ritzy for the kids, but he'd been looking forward to a meal here since deciding to come home, and after last night, he figured they deserved a treat. Besides, it was only five-fifteen. If the others got here soon, they could be finished and gone before the evening crowd came in.

Rather than hang around the marina and risk being recognized, he went straight inside.

Gabriel Mayne, owner and manager, came forward as soon as he entered, hand extended. "Arnie, I heard you were back. So good to see you."

With a grin, Arnie ignored the offered handshake and took him in a friendly hug instead. "Ah, man, it's been far too long. How are you?"

"I'm good," Gabriel said, a little stiffly.

Arnie backed off, remembering too late that Gabriel had never been a touchy-feely kind of guy. Not everyone was as comfortable with physical contact as his theatrical friends. Sometimes he forgot that.

"You're looking good," Arnie said. "Really great. I missed you when I came up in December."

"Yeah, I took off to the Canary Islands for Christmas and New Year. Got to have some time off."

At thirty-four, Gabriel and Arnie were the same age. Growing up in Nyemouth, they had gone to the same schools and had been good friends until university took them in different directions. Afterward, when Arnie had gone to London to pursue his acting dream, Gabriel had returned to Nyemouth to take his place in the family business. He'd accepted full control of the restaurant four years earlier when his parents had retired, and had raised its profile and reputation even further.

Though they had never gotten back the closeness they had enjoyed as kids, Arnie had always made a point of touching base with Gabriel when he returned to town and was proud of the way he'd modernized the traditional family restaurant and built upon its success.

Gabriel was looking good too. Six feet tall with an athletic build, his handsome home-boy looks had gotten better with age. His light brown hair was beginning to form a widow's peak, but it was cut in a short, textured style that suited him. His eyes were golden brown, and Arnie inexplicably compared them to Dominic's. Gabriel's were much lighter, less intense.

Why am I still thinking about Dominic?

As a gay, closeted teenager, Arnie had always suspected that Gabriel was the same, though they had never discussed it. They would talk with no conviction about fancying girls at school and hot women on TV. For a while, Arnie had even had a crush on his friend and swore he'd often caught Gabriel looking at him in the same way. But as two thirteen-year-old, small-town boys, they hadn't been able to bring themselves to talk about queer things, let alone admit to having those emotions.

Even now, as two openly gay men, they never talked about the feelings they'd had as teenagers. Arnie wanted to—they had so much in common, after all— but Gabriel had shut down all previous efforts he'd made to start that conversation.

So Gabriel didn't want to talk about it. Arnie was cool with that. They weren't those kids anymore.

"This place must be going well," Arnie said, staying safely on the subject of business. "I read that feature in the Sunday supplement last summer. It made me so proud. I showed it to everyone I know."

Gabriel nodded. "Yeah, that was great. We've had a couple of food critics in since then. It isn't easy enticing the big-name reviewers out of the South East, but we're getting there. We think we might have had a Michelin inspector in recently, but we won't know until they announce the guide. That would really be the making of us."

"Cool," Arnie said. "I really hope you get it."

"What about you? Anything exciting coming up?"

Arnie shrugged. "This and that. I'm just looking forward to spending the summer with my son." He was reluctant to talk about upcoming TV and film projects. It was an unpredictable business. Landing a role meant nothing until it was filmed and released. Schedules were altered, forcing a change in cast. Funding could fall through at the last minute, leading to cancelation. And completing a movie was no guarantee that it would ever be seen. Distribution deals were notoriously fragile. He'd starred in a movie three years ago that remained on the shelf to this day. And another picture he'd shot in Europe, he hadn't known they had released it until he was in a supermarket and had spotted it in the rack of budget DVDs.

His parents arrived with AJ, his sister Sophie and her kids, Conner and Indina. Conner and AJ were the same age, while Indina was two years younger. Sophie was a partner in a local firm of solicitors. She had come straight from work and still wore her business suit. Sophie was two years Arnie's senior, and she took him in a warm, protective embrace.

"How are you doing?" she asked, pressing her head against his. "My God, last night must have been awful."

"I'm fine. Don't worry. We were only witnesses."

"Even still. What a thing to see. I still can't believe that something like that happened here."

They asked Gabriel if he could give them a table at the back of the room, out of the way. The kids were high after their trip to the cinema to see a new superhero movie and Arnie didn't want them spoiling the restaurant experience for other customers. Gabriel obliged, putting them in an obscure alcove.

"Has anyone heard how the girl is doing?" Arnie asked. "Sandy, I think she's called."

"Sandy Costello," Sophie said, keeping her voice down, though the kids were engrossed in their own conversation about the movie.

"Do you know her?" Elizabeth asked.

Sophie shook her head. "I was at the police station with a client this afternoon. Everyone was talking about it. Sophie is the deputy manager of a hotel in Morpeth. The police are trying to find out more about her. She's still sedated so hasn't talked yet. They interviewed her ex-boyfriend this morning, but he has an alibi. I got the impression they were clutching at straws going after him. They've no idea why anyone would attack her."

"Maybe there was no motive," Arnie said. "Could be it was a random thing."

"Maybe," Sophie said. "They're looking into all possibilities at the moment."

"That poor girl," Elizabeth said.

Though he'd been looking forward to a meal here, Arnie found he had little appetite when the menu arrived. He opted for a loin of cod with curried vegetables and a cod skin crisp. Although it wasn't on the menu, Gabriel offered to do battered fish goujons with chips for the children.

"Perfect," Arnie said. He asked for a bottle of white wine for the adults to share and sodas for the kids. When everyone has placed their orders, he turned to his parents. "I've a bone to pick with you two. How come you didn't tell me about Dominic?"

"Tell you what?" Martin asked. "I introduced you to him last night, didn't I?"

"How about the fact he's best-selling author Jack Cole?"

"Oh, he told you, did he?"

"Dominic doesn't like to make a thing of it," Elizabeth said. "That's why he uses a pen name. To protect his identity. He doesn't let on to everybody."

"I'm hardly anybody. You could have said something. You're not exactly the souls of discretion with it comes to other people's business."

"It's up to Dominic who he wants to tell," Martin said. "He doesn't like to be treated any differently on the crew, so keeps it to himself."

"Have you read his books?"

Martin nodded. "Sure. He's a great writer. Pacey and exciting. You should try them. Whenever I start a new one, I can't put it down."

"Does he write about his career in the forces?"

"Not really. I mean, his background must inform the books, but they're all fiction. Thrillers. I don't know how much ex-service people are allowed to write about their work. Not much, I imagine. I could ask, but I don't think he would tell me. He's kind of quiet about some things."

"And kind of hot too," Sophie said. "Very."

"Sophie." Elizabeth frowned with disapproval.

"Well, he is. You'd have to be blind not to notice. Dominic Melton has got it all going on. And then some."

"Sssh," Elizabeth said, looking at the kids.

A waitress arrived with their drinks. When she had gone, Arnie asked, "How long have you known him?"

"I don't know," Martin said. "I'm terrible with dates. Seems like maybe five years. Something like that. He joined the crew soon after arriving in Nyemouth."

"That sounds about right," Elizabeth said.

It seemed strange to Arnie that they had never met before. In five years, he must have come home ten to fifteen times. How was it he'd only found out about Dominic now? Still, it had been an eventful period. He'd had enough going on in his own life to have concerned himself with the local author. The *hot* local author.

"What's his story?" he asked, trying to make his interest sound casual. "What brought him to Nyemouth? Does he have family here?"

"He never talks about them," Martin said. "I think he's pretty much on his own."

Elizabeth swept her eyes around the room, checking for eavesdroppers, before saying, "He doesn't get on with his family. I don't know why. His dad died about three years ago. I only know this because he told me just before he left for the funeral. It was somewhere in south Yorkshire and he came home straight after. Didn't even spend the night. His mother is still alive, but he doesn't seem close to her. And he had a couple of brothers. I don't think any of them bother with each other. It's sad, I think, when families don't get on."

"Not everyone is as lucky as us," Sophie said.

"You would think they'd be proud of him," Elizabeth continued. "Having done so well for himself."

"The Special Boat Service — that's a real elite group," Martin said.

"Exactly. And with the success of his books."

"That alone." Sophie laughed. "There's nothing like money for bringing estranged families back together. It's amazing what people will forgive if there's a chance of a good handout."

"I don't think the family can be hard up," Elizabeth said. "His dad was in the forces too. The RAF or something."

Arnie sipped his wine. The more he heard about Dominic, the more interested he became. There were so many fascinating things about him, so much of interest. His career, his writing. Why he'd chosen to settle in Nyemouth having had no obvious connection to the town.

You're not interested, remember. Romance is not an option. There was no reason they couldn't be friends. Dominic seemed like a cool guy and Arnie could do with a friend in town. Things weren't the same between him and Gabriel as they'd been when they were young. They got on well enough, always made time to chat and catch up, but there was a distance between them. There had been ever since they'd gone their separate ways as teenagers, and Arnie couldn't see them being close again. He'd love it if they could. He was willing, but after Gabriel's reaction to his earlier embrace, he doubted the feeling was mutual.

So why not reach out to Dominic? In a friendly, platonic way. They were close to the same age and bound to have a lot in common. Why shouldn't they be buddies?

Because you want to fuck his brains out!

When Dominic looked as hot as he did, what were the chances of Arnie maintaining a physical and emotional distance? *Zero.*

It would be impossible not to fancy him. Unless he turned out to be the biggest arsehole in town—and judging by how rapturously his parents spoke about him, that was unlikely—Arnie would be fated to fall in love with him.

Would that really be such a bad thing? Couldn't I use some excitement in my life? Yes. No. Maybe.

"At least Dominic isn't all by himself," Elizabeth said.

Arnie froze, the wineglass halfway to his lips. "What do you mean?"

"Gabriel," she said, nodding across the restaurant to his old schoolmate. "He and Dominic have been seeing each other. They've been trying to keep it hush hush, but a few people have seen them together. They make a beautiful couple, don't you think?"

Chapter Six

Dominic Melton drove into the hard body beneath him. The bed squeaked as he increased his pace, desperate for release. It had been a long time coming — too long. He'd come close twice already, but something kept him from a climax. Gritting his teeth, he shoved his arms under Gabriel's chest. He gripped him tight and pounded harder. Gabriel's skin glistened with sweat. Dominic had to hold him tighter to stop from slipping off. He pressed his face against the back of Gabriel's head, pushing him into the pillow, inhaling the scent of his hair.

It was no good.

Gabriel was no good.

He wasn't the man he wanted.

Dominic closed his eyes, forcing all thoughts of Gabriel from his mind, focusing on one thing — Arnie Walker. It was Arnie beneath him now. Facedown, hot, slippery and willing. Dominic let out a desperate cry with each inward thrust.

Driving into Arnie. Giving it to his arse. Getting close. Closer. Yes. *Yes.* With a final cry that sounded close to rage, he was there.

After all the effort, the orgasm was frustratingly weak.

"Are you okay?" he asked, breathless, knowing that the man beneath him was Gabriel and not Arnie Walker. He held the base of his cock, keeping the condom in place, and withdrew.

Gabriel rolled onto his back, presenting his hard dick. Dominic took it in an obliging grip and jerked until Gabriel squirted a copious load across his taut abs.

"Oh fuck," he sighed, putting a hand on Dominic's wrist to halt the action. "No more."

Gabriel wanted to cuddle afterward. He always did.

"I need to get rid of this," Dominic said, easing off the condom and wrapping it in a wad of tissues. He handed the box to Gabriel before striding naked to the bathroom. He disposed of the rubber and wiped the sweat from his face with a towel, avoiding his reflection in the mirror.

Why did you do that? This isn't worth it.

He'd been trying to cut back on these sessions with Gabriel. It had started well enough. A casual agreement between two single men. Gabriel was attractive and the sex had been fun. That was all Dominic was interested in—a no-strings-attached fuck buddy. They used to get together every couple of weeks and that was that.

When Gabriel had suggested they meet up more often, it had seemed harmless enough. Why not? The sex *was* good, after all. As long as it didn't interfere with his writing or lifeboat commitments, he saw no harm in it.

It had taken some time to realize Gabriel wanted more. The situation had been so easy, so convenient, that he'd thought nothing of it when Gabriel's booty calls occurred two or three times a week. It wasn't until he'd started texting about non-sex-related things and calling round with food and drink that it had become obvious Gabriel viewed their hook-ups more seriously than he did.

Dominic had made his intentions very clear—he wasn't in the market for a relationship. Gabriel had insisted he felt the same, that Dominic had read things wrong. He didn't want a boyfriend either, just a good fuck now and then. However, Dominic had seen a lot less of him lately. He hadn't kept count, but it must have been a good month since their last hook-up. Tonight wouldn't have happened if Gabriel hadn't texted him after a couple of scotches. In a moment of weakness, he'd said yes.

The minute they were naked, Dominic had known he'd made a mistake. Gabriel had been all over him, needy and impatient. Dominic didn't want him. He'd known in an instant the fire had gone out, but he'd gone through with it just the same.

When he returned to the bedroom, Gabriel lay naked on top of the covers and showed no inclination to move. Most men would be grateful. With his toned figure and his hairy chest and legs, Gabriel was a knock-out—physically perfect. He was smart too, with a great knowledge of the local area and history. Friendly and successful, perfect boyfriend material.

For someone else.

Dominic liked him all right, but there was nothing deeper between them. He saw Gabriel as a friend. Take away the sex and they got on as well as he did with any of his buddies in the lifeboat crew. Only Gabriel seemed to want more.

It had gone midnight. Dominic wanted to take Brandy for a quick walk then get back to bed, alone. He retrieved his underpants from the floor and pulled them on, hoping Gabriel would take the hint.

"Arnie Walker came into the restaurant tonight," Gabriel said, gazing at the ceiling, seemingly content where he was. "I haven't seen him in a while."

Dominic put on his jeans. "Yeah? He dropped by the station this afternoon. He seems like a nice guy."

"That's his thing, isn't it? The all-round nice guy. He's made a career out of that act."

Dominic ignored the catty tone of Gabriel's voice. "How well do you know him?"

"We were at school together. We're the same age."

"So, what's wrong? Didn't the two of you get along?"

"No. We were friends. Good friends, as it happened. I just think, oh, I don't know, that he got too big in the head for this place. He waltzes home once or twice a year and the town is expected to roll out the red carpet, like he's visiting royalty, or something."

Dominic frowned. "That's not the impression I got. In fact, he seemed very down to earth. Not at all stuck up."

Gabriel huffed. "He's not as grand as he used to be, that's true. But his career isn't as big as it once was. The Hollywood movies and all that are a thing of the past. He's no longer the big-I-am and has to slum it in TV and crappy British films."

"Now you're just being bitchy," Dominic said, finding his socks and sitting on the edge of the bed to put them on. "I've not found anyone who has a bad thing to say about him. Until now."

"You wouldn't. The whole town worships him. Like the sun shines out of his arse. He's their golden boy."

Dominic smiled and shook his head. He recognized Gabriel's words for what they were — jealousy. Unfounded at that. Gabriel had done well. His business was a massive success. In a town like Nyemouth, that was a big thing. He shouldn't compare it to the career of a famous actor. Gabriel didn't need to measure his accomplishments against Arnie. They had both achieved great things in different areas.

"What was he like at school?" he asked.

"All right, I suppose. We were friends and used to play together. His mother owned a guest house and my parents had the restaurant, so we had a lot in common. I think we just drifted apart when he got into the drama and all that. It wasn't for me."

"And you were both gay? That must have been a major bond. Most teenagers have to go through that alone."

Gabriel rolled onto his side, rising onto an elbow to look at him. "I didn't know he was gay. Not really. I suspected, but we never discussed it. When he went off and got married, I assumed I'd been mistaken or that it was wishful thinking on my part."

"Doesn't it strike you as odd? That you were both gay and didn't know it?"

"We were teenagers. We didn't have those kinds of conversations. It was kind of shy and awkward. We used to talk about girls and pretend to fancy them."

"But you really fancied Arnie?"

"Absolutely I did. He was hot, even then. I think I was around sixteen or seventeen before I started to fill out and look pretty decent, but Arnie was always huge and looked like a man at fourteen. No one dared to pick on him, that's for sure. I used to look at his body when we were on the beach. At first, I think I convinced myself that I was curious about him, about how much more mature and muscular he was than me. It didn't take long to realize I wasn't *curious* about his body. I *wanted* it."

"Why didn't you do something about it? Make a move on him?"

"I wouldn't have dared. I doubt he would either. We weren't open to things like that. You read about that kind of stuff in books, best friends fooling around together. I doubt it happens much in reality."

"So, he was your best friend?"

Gabriel looked thoughtful and took his time before answering. "I suppose he was. Yes, the best friend I ever had. Even though we didn't do more than hang out. I spent more time with Arnie than anyone else."

"So, what's your beef with him? You talk like you hate him."

He shrugged. "I don't *dislike* him. I could never say that. I guess I just resent him a little. For leaving Nyemouth."

"I thought you liked it here."

"I do," he said. "I love it. I've known nothing else. Even when I went to uni, it was with the expectation that I would come home and run the family business. Arnie never had that. No one expected him to return and take over the B&B. He made his own choices. And now he has the best of both worlds. He has his life and career in London and returns to Nyemouth once or twice a year for a hero's welcome."

Dominic struggled to believe him. It was sourness talking. He'd seen nothing in the last few days to suggest local people treated him as anything special. No one had made a big deal last night or this afternoon. Dominic had always been a good detector of bullshit and Gabriel's pettiness sounded like exactly that.

"It's getting late," he said, buttoning his shirt. "I need to walk Brandy before bed."

Though he looked surprised, Gabriel took the hint. They had only spent the night together a couple of times. Agreeing to this impromptu booty call had been a mistake and letting Gabriel stay would give him the wrong impression.

As he watched Gabriel search for his clothes, Dominic knew this would be their last liaison.

* * * *

Brandy took her time, sniffing the bushes along the cliff path. Dominic didn't mind. He was in no hurry. It was a beautiful night, far different from twenty-four hours earlier. The sky was clear and littered with stars, while the sea made a gentle hushing sound as it washed over the shore. He gazed out into the inky blackness and filled his lungs with the refreshing salty air.

It was moments like this that made him appreciate his life right now. Calm and peaceful. He'd seen plenty of action in his time, so much danger and destruction, and had reached a stage where he no longer needed that.

This was everything. The sea, the nights, the coastal town where he had made his home. So he might have no one to share it with—he didn't care about that. He had friends, his dog, his house, the lifeboat. Maybe romance would come his way in time. Maybe it wouldn't. He'd lived without it all his life. He couldn't miss what he'd never had.

Brandy trotted over to announce that she was done. He used the flashlight on his phone to clean up after her and they headed back along the path toward his house.

There was a lamp on in Jacob's living room. His friend did not sleep much these days. Dominic could call in and the old man would be glad to see him, but he decided against it. It was already late. If he went inside, he knew they would end up drinking more than was good for them.

Maybe another night.

In bed, he found it hard to sleep. The sheets smelled of Gabriel. He would change them in the morning. Gabriel was a nice guy — he just wasn't the guy for Dominic.

He reached for his tablet at the side of the bed and opened Netflix. He entered Arnie's name into the search function. There were three results — a five-year-old action film, a period drama and a TV series in which he appeared to play a doctor being stalked by a patient. The action piece sounded like the easiest watch.

Dominic settled down with the tablet on his chest. He drifted off to sleep watching Arnie Walker and dreamed about him a lot that night.

Chapter Seven

On Friday morning, Arnie sat in the shade of the veranda while AJ played with his cousins Conner and Indina and their black Lab, Benji, at the bottom of the garden. He'd volunteered for babysitting duties most of this week and had enjoyed it tremendously. The kids provided a necessary distraction. Since Monday evening, the press had been on his case. The attack on Sandy Costello was big news and reporters had inundated the town, looking for a story.

Sandy had sustained horrific injuries in the fall, and when Arnie had checked with the hospital last night, she remained in an induced coma. There were fractures to her head, neck, back, arms, pelvis and legs. The official stance from her doctors was that she was in a stable condition. Arnie knew that was a massive understatement. If she pulled through this, the damage to her body would be life-changing.

And at the moment that was still a huge *if*.

They had made no arrests. The police were keeping their investigation quiet, but Arnie had heard from the best source in town—his mother—that they were getting nowhere. They had interviewed Sandy's friends, family, colleagues and ex-boyfriends, and so far, there were no suspects. She was a hard-working, well-liked regular woman with no obvious enemies. It looked increasingly likely that the attack had been a random incident.

It could have happened to anyone. Arnie got chills every time he thought about that fact. How easily it could have been AJ.

He had kept his son close to him all week.

The photographers on their doorstep had forced them to stay home a lot. Fortunately, there was plenty of privacy at the back of the house. The courtyard and garden could not be seen from the road. Arnie had gone on lockdown to look after the kids.

By the end of the week, interest in him and the story appeared to have waned. With no arrest, no new developments or, God forbid, no further attacks, the press moved on. When he'd looked out that morning, the road had been clear. If no one turned up by the time they'd had lunch, he intended to take the kids out for the afternoon.

Although the confinement had been enforced, Arnie had enjoyed these quiet few days at home. It was a rare treat to sit still this long. The kids amused themselves playing in the garden, or with video games indoors. All he had to do was lie back and keep an eye on them. He loved it.

AJ, Conner and Indina threw a Frisbee around the garden. The dog ran after them to begin with but had grown tired of their endless energy and sought shelter in the shade of the cherry tree. With a smile, Arnie returned his attention to a well-read paperback.

Hard to Kill by Jack Cole, aka Dominic Melton. The book was a major page turner.

He'd begun reading on Wednesday night before bed and had less than a quarter remaining. He'd always avoided this kind of espionage thriller in the past, worried they would be too complicated and technical for him to follow. Previously he'd appeared in whole films where he didn't understand the convoluted machinations of the plot. He'd turn up and say the lines in the hope it would make sense to someone eventually. But he couldn't have been more wrong about Dominic's novel. The writing style was crisp and clean. The story took some labyrinthine turns and it was riddled with deceit and double-crosses, yet Arnie never got lost.

The action scenes were exciting. He wondered, as he read, how much of it was based on Dominic's own experiences in the Marines and Special Boat Service. Maybe not directly — the book was fiction, after all — but Dominic wrote with the confident voice of experience. He had a talent for grabbing the reader and pulling them along for the ride.

It was a pity there was no author photo on the cover, for no other reason than Arnie wanted to look at him. Dominic used a pen name to protect his anonymity, therefore it was obvious he wouldn't want his face on the jacket. Still, Arnie would have liked a tiny piece of him.

Dominic Melton was not on social media. Arnie had checked. No Facebook, Twitter or Instagram. Jack Cole had a website and social accounts. All pretty anonymous, book-related stuff. One look and Arnie knew the publicity department of his publisher managed the account. There were flurries of posts around the time of each new release then nothing more for months afterward.

It fit with the impression of the man he had met. Strong, dark, independent. He wouldn't seek validation through followers or likes. His life was full. He had huge success with his work, the excitement of serving in the lifeboat and a hot man in Gabriel.

Yes, Gabriel. Dominic is taken. It was a blessing for sure. Though Arnie told himself he wasn't interested in any kind of relationship, in truth he thought about Dominic far too much. It was the beginning of an infatuation.

But Dominic was with Gabriel, so Arnie had to stay well away.

And he would.

He read for half an hour and was thoroughly engrossed in the book when AJ came over. The boy's face was flushed and glistened with sweat.

"What time is lunch?" he asked.

Arnie glanced at his watch. It was almost one. "Whenever you want it? You hungry now?"

AJ nodded. "Can we have chicken nuggets?"

"Maybe tonight. Not for lunch. You can have tuna or turkey. What's it to be?"

"Turkey," he said happily.

"Okay then." Arnie marked his place in the book and got up. "I'll call you when it's ready."

From the kitchen, he could see through the open French doors into the garden and keep an eye on them. They had resumed their game with the Frisbee. Before starting on lunch, he went to the front door and looked out. The road remained clear. No reporters, no photographers. They must have given up, realizing there was no story or photo opportunity to be had.

Now he could take the kids out for the afternoon. Maybe to the cinema or the swimming baths. He'd see how they all felt after lunch.

Back in the kitchen, he checked his phone. There were several text messages. Nothing that looked important. He read the one from Sophie in case it related to Conner or Indina.

Have you seen the state of your ex in the papers today? The woman has no class.

Sophie had attached a link to save him searching for the story. Arnie had little interest in what Tara did these days, but he had to keep up with her trash stories in order to screen them from AJ.

Breast of Friends, the headline screamed. The photos that accompanied the article told him enough — he didn't have to read the rest. Tara and Richie had been papped at a pool party in Ibiza. Tara cavorted topless in a Jacuzzi with another bare-breasted woman while Richie looked on. Each picture was more lurid than the one before. Tara and the woman laughed and pushed their silicone-enhanced boobs together as Richie poured champagne over them. Richie's red shorts could not conceal his obvious hard-on.

Tara looked awful in all the pictures. She was bloated and boozy, with ratty hair and makeup smeared across her face. She'd gone up a breast size since meeting Richie, and the captions that accompanied each picture read *Making a Tit of Herself* and *Bosom Buddies*. They were obviously high as well as drunk. Tara had a glassy, faraway, dead-behind-the-eyes look in every shot.

It was easy for the press to snap unflattering photographs of celebrities and ridicule them in print, but Tara and Richie made no effort to protect themselves. They reveled in the attention, no matter how negative or disagreeable it got.

"Is it ready yet?"

The appearance of three kids at the French doors startled him. He shoved his phone into his pocket.

"Coming right up," he said with a smile. "Wash your hands and set the table. The sandwiches will soon be ready. Turkey for everyone?"

"Yay." All three of them answered at once.

They were so pure and innocent. It often felt like a losing battle trying to protect them from the harsh realities of the world.

* * * *

On the south side of the river, Dominic hit save on the document he'd been working on and put his laptop to sleep. It had been a productive morning. He'd written one thousand eight hundred words of his latest novel. Only two hundred short of his daily target. It wouldn't take him long to reach it. He forced himself to write two thousand words a day, Monday to Friday. No excuses, whether it took till midday or six p.m., he wouldn't pack up until he hit it.

He sat back in his chair and sighed, stretching his aching back and shoulders.

He had converted the second bedroom into an office. With a large oak desk and crammed bookcases, it was one of his favorite rooms in the house. It certainly had the best view, looking straight down the garden to the open sea. He looked out of the window at a perfect afternoon, cobalt-blue water with just a gentle swell, and a cloudless sky. When he finished his work, he would treat Brandy to a long stroll along the cliffs.

Dominic went to the bathroom and washed his hands. Jacob had invited him for lunch. His neighbor had come by early that morning to collect Brandy. He often took the dog on his morning walk into town to pick up a newspaper. On his return around eight o'clock, the old man had excitedly showed him a bulging carrier bag of freshly caught crabs.

"I saw one of the boats coming in and hung around to see what they had." He'd beamed. "Come for lunch around one. They don't get much fresher than this."

* * * *

Dominic smelled the delicious aroma of boiled crabs as he walked up the front path. Jacob had been busy. He'd cooked, shelled and picked clean eight crabs, separating the meat into containers of white and brown flesh.

"Set the table outside," he called as Dominic entered. "It's a lovely day. We might as well enjoy it."

They ate on the small front terrace, overlooking the bay. The crab meat was delicious. Jacob served the sweet white flesh with a simple salad and crusty white bread. Dominic added olive oil and vinegar to his.

"This makes a change from the usual tuna sandwich," Dominic said as he finished mopping his plate with bread to ensure nothing was wasted.

"I'll say it does. Stroke of luck to be there just as the boat came in. Most of the catch has gone off to market by the time I usually get down there. And that stuff they sell in the supermarket is days if not weeks old."

Dominic told Jacob to sit and enjoy the sun while he cleared away afterward. He loaded the dishwasher and returned to the terrace with two cups of tea — good and strong, just how Jacob liked it.

"Arnie's ex-wife has been making a spectacle of herself again," Jacob said, handing over the newspaper he'd been reading.

Dominic's eyes widened as he saw the double-page spread. He'd never heard of Tara Westmoorland-Hughes until earlier this week. He found it hard to believe her drunken exploits were so newsworthy, yet here she was with her tits unfurled across pages four and five. The woman and her friends in the picture were out of it. *What a mess.*

He looked at the photos of her new husband with interest. Drugs and alcohol must have destroyed her judgement, because Richie Hughes was no Arnie Walker. He'd never heard of Richie or Loctite, the indie-rock band he fronted. While idly searching online for info about Arnie, he'd learned that Richie's working-class, hard-man-of-rock persona was just an act. He came from a privileged, upper-class family. He was nothing more than a rich kid trying to live the 'sex, drugs and rock-and-roll' lifestyle. Richie had greasy, shoulder-length hair, a multitude of ugly tattoos and a starvation-thin figure. He might be having a high old time, but the drugs had ruined what looks he used to have.

Tara's standards couldn't have fallen more dramatically. From the godly Arnie to a sewer rat like Richie.

"Have you seen anything of Arnie this week?" Dominic tried to make the question sound casual.

Jacob shook his head. "Saw his dad yesterday. According to Martin, Arnie has been keeping a low profile, what with all the press people hanging around town. Can't say I blame him, especially with the way Tara is carrying on. But it looks like things might be calming down here. I didn't notice any of those newspaper folks this morning."

"I couldn't do it. Being followed around like that, never sure where the cameras are lurking."

"You're used to lying low and keeping hidden. It's second nature to you. People like Tara are just the opposite. It seemed like life isn't worth living unless it's in front of a camera. I think she might come to regret that in time. She can't take those pictures back, after all. I expect Arnie will do all he can to keep them from AJ, but the boy will see them eventually. Maybe not today, but when he goes back to school, you can be sure some little shit will fall over themselves to show him."

Dominic folded the paper and pushed it away. "I've been watching one of Arnie's TV shows on Netflix. The one where he played a doctor." Dominic seldom made time for television, but across the week he'd committed to watching Arnie every night. The show was gripping and had become a regular part of his nightly routine, enjoying an episode of the six-part series before bed.

The writing was first-rate, with a story full of intrigue and suspense, and at the heart of the show was Arnie's compelling performance of a man trapped in a nightmare situation.

"That's a good one," Jacob said. "I can't believe you haven't seen it already. Everyone was talking about that when it went out."

"Don't spoil it for me. I've got two episodes left to go."

Jacob sipped his tea, watching Dominic across the rim of the mug. "You like him, don't you?"

He shrugged. "I don't know him."

Jacob chuckled. "Then I'll rephrase it. You fancy him. Would that be more accurate?"

Now Dominic laughed. "It would be hard not to fancy him. He's beautiful."

"So, what's the problem? Go on, ask him out. He won't eat you."

"I already told you. He's famous. I can't be bothered with all that crap." He gestured to the newspaper. "I'm not going to be tomorrow's news. Like Tara and what's-his-face."

"Arnie isn't like that. That's all Tara. He's never been interested in the publicity."

"Yes, but the press is interested in him. Didn't you just tell me he's been hiding all week to avoid them? I don't want to get mixed up in that. I like my life as it is. Simple."

"And alone."

"But not lonely. I've got you. I've got Brandy. Friends. The lifeboat."

"That's not the same and you know it. I think you are lonely in that house by yourself. I know I am in here. You need someone. You deserve more than an old man and a dog."

"I don't need an actor. Or a guy with an ex-wife who's all over the papers on a daily basis."

"Don't be so judgmental," Jacob said. "You don't even know the man, and you never will unless you make the effort. Take him for a drink and a bite to eat. You might get a pleasant surprise. And it's better than one of your booty calls with Gabriel Mayne."

He laughed. "What do you know about booty calls?"

"That's what it is, isn't it? You and Gabriel."

"You could say that."

"I *am* saying it. So, you've got nothing to lose in asking Arnie out."

"I've told you, I don't know him. I can hardly go knocking on his door. He's got a kid."

Jacob tutted. "You're making excuses. Bad ones at that. This weekend is the lifeboat fair. Arnie will be there with his family. Ask him then."

"And what if he says no?"

Jacob grinned. "I don't think he will. You guys will be perfect together. I know it, and I'm never wrong."

* * * *

Arnie took a sip of red wine before setting his glass on the side of the huge bath and dipping his shoulders beneath the foaming water. This was a luxury, being able to stretch out in a tub. His height meant he often had to sit with a straight back and his knees bent. The tub was massive, and he intended to enjoy it as much as possible while they were here.

AJ was in bed, fast asleep, blissfully exhausted after a day with his cousins and their dog. Arnie felt pretty tired too. He'd underestimated how much effort it required to take care of three kids, being used to only one.

After lunch that day, he'd bundled them all into the car and driven south, down the coast, stopping at some of the towns and villages he used to enjoy as a kid himself, places he hadn't revisited in years. He'd taken them for a walk along the beach at Newbiggin by the Sea, before enjoying ice-creams at the Italian café that had been on the promenade since his dad was a boy.

On the way back, they'd stopped on the outskirts of the town, before returning to Nyemouth.

AJ had insisted on picking up chicken nuggets for dinner. Arnie had relented, figuring they'd all had a decent amount of exercise for one day. When he'd put the boy to bed, he'd seemed to fall asleep as soon as the covers were drawn over him.

He had seen no reporters and hoped they'd gone for good. There had been a hairy moment in the café when he'd realized someone at the next table had left a newspaper open on the topless pictures of Tara. He'd managed to distract the kids while he'd gotten rid of it. Despite such minor hiccups, it had been an enjoyable day.

He prayed it would continue and he could give AJ the carefree summer he deserved.

No more stress. No more violence. They'd had enough to last a lifetime.

Arnie sighed and sank lower, allowing the water to come all the way up to his chin.

His thoughts turned to Dominic Melton. It seemed he was rarely ever out of them. He had around three chapters remaining of *Hard to Kill*. When he got out of the bath, Arnie planned to do nothing more than slide into bed and finish the novel. Though he was tired from his day with the kids, he knew he wouldn't sleep until he was done with the book. It was the most exciting thing he had ever read.

No surprise, when it was written by the most exciting man he'd ever met.

Really?

Yes.

It was true. None of the men he'd encountered on film sets or in TV studios came close. No matter how good-looking, none of them had what he had. Not even the stuntmen, who were some of the toughest guys he knew.

What Dominic did, what all lifeboat volunteers did, required fearlessness. There were no safety wires or standby teams when they went on a rescue. The danger was real. It took guts and bravery to go out in those boats.

And Dominic had those smoldering good looks to go with his bravery. He was a complete package.

He also has a boyfriend. Your oldest friend.

That put him out of bounds. There'd been too many secret relationships in Arnie's past. All those years he'd spent in the closet, married to Tara while sneaking around with other men, many of whom had wives and girlfriends of their own. Or the star fuckers — guys who were prepared to forget their other halves for an hour or two so they could make it with a celebrity.

Arnie had been so desperate to make contact with other guys back then that he'd made mistakes and gotten involved with a number of wrong men. None of it had made him happy. His days of twenty- and thirty-percent relationships — of making do — were over.

He wanted a man who could give him one hundred percent. No sharing.

Pity, when Dominic was perfect in every other way.

Arnie ran his hands across his body beneath the water. Thinking about Dominic gave him an erection. It seemed to happen every time. The fact that Dominic was in a relationship with Gabriel did nothing to quell his sexiness. Arnie wouldn't ever make a move on him — no chance. It didn't mean he couldn't think about him now and then, even fantasize a little.

He wrapped his hand around his engorged dick. He hadn't beaten it in days, maybe the best part of two weeks. His balls ached and thinking about Dominic meant he was very horny. If he couldn't have the real thing, he could at least do something about this.

Arnie raised his head. He'd left the door ajar so he could hear if AJ got out of bed. Silence. The boy had been fast asleep last time he checked.

Settling back into the water, he took his cock in a firm grip. He moved his left hand lower and tugged his balls, enjoying the tension. He closed his eyes, easily envisioning Dominic, imaging that perfect face coming close to his, their lips touching. Gently to begin with, before moving deeper into the kiss. He could almost feel it, Dominic's mouth on his, inhaling his hot breath.

He moved his hands faster, slipping the foreskin back and forth over the head. It had been far too long. The sensation was exquisite, each stroke building the pleasure. He moved his other hand lower, behind his balls, reaching between his thighs, to the tight cleft of his anus. He found the opening and pressed, groaning as he imagined Dominic touching him there, probing, exploring, entering him. Arnie gasped, pushing his feet against the far side of the bath. Hot water and foam splashed and spilled over the sides. He jerked his hand faster and faster until he could take no more.

"Dominic." He sighed as he came.

Afterward, cleaned up and toweled dry, Arnie put on a robe and carried his wine glass to the master bedroom. He felt better, having released some of the frustration he felt about Dominic, and a lot of the tension that had built in him this week. It was surprising how things crept up.

Now he looked forward to finishing *Hard to Kill* and getting a good night's sleep.

He went to check on AJ before turning in. He'd already locked up downstairs and had set the alarm before taking his bath. Standing outside his son's bedroom, he listened to the reassuring rhythm of his breath. Satisfied, he crossed to the landing window to take a look out the front.

The motion detector spotlight that covered the front of the property was on, illuminating the path and the road beyond. Arnie pressed his face to the window and looked thoroughly in both directions. There were no cars parked outside, no people walking past and most importantly no reporters.

It was probably nothing, he reasoned. A passing vehicle, or a cat, maybe a fox could have activated the light. They were in the country here, sharing the space with nature. He couldn't take alarm at such minor incidents.

One last look verified there was nobody there.

Convinced, he turned out the hall light and headed for the bedroom.

He had a date with Dominic Melton, aka Jack Cole, and the final few pages of *Hard to Kill*. Not as good as the real thing, he was sure, but it was better than nothing.

* * * *

Across the road, a figure lurked in the shadows. The range of Arnie Walker's security light did not stretch this far. On the open grassland, leading to the edge of the cliff, the darkness was complete. From there the figure had watched the house unseen as Arnie had come to the window.

So, Arnie is security conscious. Point duly noted.

The house at night would be hard to enter undetected. Difficult. Not impossible. Nothing was impossible for someone well prepared. That was what tonight was about, after all. Surveillance. Preparation.

The time for action would come.

And when it did, Arnie Walker would never see it coming.

Chapter Eight

"Dad, can I get my face painted? *Please.*"

AJ stared with wide eyes as a boy about his age walked by with his face made up as a lion.

It was Sunday afternoon and the annual lifeboat fair, a large-scale gala designed to raise money for the station, as well as its profile. The fair had been a Nyemouth tradition for as long as Arnie could remember, though he couldn't recall there ever being as big a crowd as had turned out today. The weather played a large part in it. It was a glorious day and would have brought hundreds of tourists to the town without the draw of the fair. Arnie suspected the dramatic rescue of Sandy Costello last weekend, together with the national publicity it had generated, was another contributing factor to the increased attendance.

For some it would be idle curiosity, a chance to see the town and the boat that had featured in the headlines. Arnie liked to think that most people had been drawn by a desire to contribute to the worthy cause. Either way, as long as they spent money, it was all good.

The marina and the surrounding streets were adorned with flags and bunting. There were stalls set up around the station, selling cakes, homemade jams, official merchandise and used goods. There were tombolas and raffles and volunteers moving through the crowds with collecting buckets. They had erected a stage where local bands played live music and there were pop-up fast food stalls and ice cream vans. Beyond the waterfront, they had turned the town square into an amusement park with fun rides and games. Everyone was doing good business.

Arnie held AJ's hand as they made their way into the square in search of the face-painting stall. He didn't want to lose him in the crowd. He knew it would be impossible for them to go unrecognized today, given all the publicity this week, but he'd been determined they would not miss the fair. It was too important for them to stay away. He endeavored to keep a low profile, dressed in navy chino shorts and deck shoes, a white linen shirt, straw hat and shades. Apart from his towering height, he looked like dozens of other guys milling through the crowd.

They had recognized him, though. People smiled and said hello, others pointed and stared, but there had been no trouble. He returned the smiles, waved and kept moving. Most folk seemed to appreciate that he was with his son and left them alone.

"Oh no," AJ said when they located the face-painting artists. "There's a queue."

"Well," Arnie informed him, "if this is what you want, you have to wait your turn. Is it?"

AJ nodded enthusiastically.

"Okay, let's join the queue."

It was lucky, he thought, not for the first time, that AJ's temperament was more like his own than his mother. Tara didn't believe in waiting for anything. She considered celebrity status, however minor, gave someone rights above ordinary people. She used her fame to push, bully, snatch and grab her way through life. It would kill him should AJ grow up to have principles like that.

Arnie did his best to raise him with the attitude that everything had to be earned.

There were three face-painting artists on the stall and the queue moved fast. Within twenty minutes AJ stood proudly before him, made up as a tiger. He growled and hooked his hands into claws.

Arnie laughed. He was so cute. He got out his phone and took several photos while AJ crouched and snarled, completely into the part.

"Now what?" Arnie asked.

"Let's go and show Grandma."

"Grandma is working today." His mother was running the merchandise stall outside the station.

"She'll still want to see me. C'mon."

AJ grabbed his hand and pulled him back toward the waterfront. More people had arrived and the town was swarming. The lifeboat must be well on the way to an afternoon of record takings. They needed it badly. The public only had so much money to go around and the boat was often overlooked, forgotten until someone required the service. He understood why people were more willing to donate to hospitals and children's charities — he supported those causes himself, which made days like this so important. Every penny collected was essential.

Slowly, they picked their way through the crowd to the station.

"Grandma, Grandma," AJ shouted, rushing to her stall to show off his tiger face.

Elizabeth squealed with delight and told him how fierce he looked, before snapping some photos on her phone. AJ growled and adopted tiger poses. The boy was a natural performer.

"How's it going?" Arnie asked.

"Excellent," Elizabeth said. "We've already beaten last year's total."

There were four other people behind the long merchandise stall, all busy as customers bought tea towels, toys, stationery and Christmas cards.

"Do you guys want anything?" he asked. "I can cover while you take a break?"

"You could get us some more cold drinks," she said. "It's roasting out here."

They had taken the lifeboat out of the station for the day and the interior was being used as pop-up café. As Arnie joined the line to buy drinks, he felt a tap on his shoulder. It was his sister Sophie and her husband, Cyrus. He kissed Sophie on the cheek, while Cyrus, wary of a hug, thrust his hand forward for a shake.

"Arnie," he said curtly. His handshake was stiff and unnecessarily tight.

Cyrus was an exceptionally good-looking black man in his late thirties. Sophie had met him in her last year of university, and they'd been together since then. In the early days of their relationship, Arnie had gotten on well with him. Cyrus had been good-natured and funny back then.

A lot had changed. Cyrus worked at a law firm in Newcastle, and as his career took off, he became increasingly arrogant. Working in a cut-throat, city-center business had made him harder and less friendly, and he'd become aloof around Arnie, especially since Arnie had gained full-time custody of AJ.

Arnie had never asked Sophie about it, but suspected her husband had issues regarding an openly gay man raising a child. Either that, or he was such an alpha-male that he couldn't handle the fact that his queer brother-in-law was wealthier than him. Toxic masculinity or outright homophobia — Arnie couldn't decide what Cyrus' problem was. Either way, he had no time for his bullshit.

"Cyrus," he replied. "It's been a long time." When Arnie and AJ had come to visit last Christmas, his brother-in-law had had numerous excuses to avoid all the family events they'd attended. Arnie resolved not to let him off the hook so easily today. "How are things with you?" he asked, the question directed at Cyrus.

"All good," he replied, avoiding eye contact.

"Is work going well?" Arnie persisted.

"Brilliant. I'm a senior partner now."

"Yes. I'd heard that. Congratulations. You must be very pleased."

"I work more hours than anyone else at the firm. I'm the highest earner. I deserve it." Finally, Cyrus looked Arnie in the eye. "I'm buying a motorboat, a yacht, to celebrate."

"Okay," Arnie said, bemused.

"Cyrus has always wanted his own boat," Sophie said. The joy in her voice struck a false note.

"I'll moor her in the South of France," he said, animated now that he had something to brag about. "We'll sail her around the Med. Spain, France, Italy. I can't wait to take her to Portofino. It's one of the most spectacular harbours in the world."

As are the billionaire super-yachts that moor there. He didn't know what kind of boat Cyrus intended to buy, but he knew it would not be in that class. "I'm pleased for you. I just hope you've factored the time off into your busy schedule. There's no point owning a yacht when you're all about work and no play, is there?"

Cyrus' nostrils flared. "It's stuffy in here. I can't bear it. I'll wait outside." He turned his back on Arnie and headed for the door.

"Where's AJ?" Sophie asked, overly bright, as though her husband hadn't just served her brother a huge diss.

"Outside with Mam. I'm just getting drinks for everyone."

"We're taking the kids on a boat ride. There's an old steamer in the harbour running trips. It takes about an hour and the next one leaves at four. Do you think AJ would like to come?"

Arnie knew his son would enjoy the adventure of a boat trip, but he didn't like the idea of spending five minutes at sea with Cyrus, let alone a full hour.

As though reading his mind, Sophie added, "You don't have to come. We'll take AJ off your hands for a few hours. It's the least we can do after all the free child-minding you've done this week. How about it? It'll give you the chance to relax for a while. You could go for a pint. Enjoy the sun."

The idea had its merits. "All right," he said. "If AJ wants to go, that would be great."

When he reached the front of the line, Arnie bought a dozen cans of Diet Coke and, with Sophie's help, carried them to his mother's stall. AJ leapt at the chance to join his cousins on the boat trip. Arnie gave him money for the fare and any snacks he wanted onboard.

"I'll tell you what," Sophie said. "We'll take them all for something to eat when we get back ashore. That'll give you a few more hours' peace. How about we drop him at the house around seven thirty?"

AJ and the other kids looked thrilled by her suggestion, Cyrus a lot less so. Arnie tried to give her some extra cash to cover AJ's dinner, but Sophie refused to take it, saying it was her treat. As she took the kids toward the pier, Arnie found himself with time to kill.

Now what?

The fair would run for at least another hour before winding down. Knowing his mother, as long as there were people around the station, she would keep her stall open. His dad was somewhere in the crowd with a collection bucket. Sophie's idea of getting a drink and enjoying the afternoon sun seemed like a good suggestion. He decided to take a walk around the marina first.

He'd seen nothing of Dominic since arriving. There was no reason that he should have. For the crew and volunteers, the fair meant constant work. Whether running a stall or an information booth, or getting into the crowd with a collection bucket, there was a job for everyone. Dominic would be out there, doing whatever it took to raise money, making him near impossible to locate on a busy day like this.

The waterfront was as packed as everywhere else. He managed to squeeze to the front in time to see AJ and his cousins board the tourist boat with Sophie and Cyrus. He ran excitedly to the bow of the craft, still beaming with his tiger face. Arnie laughed and tried to take some photos, though they were too far away for anything decent to come out.

Behind him, someone said, "Look, there's Arnie Walker. The guy in the straw hat."

Time to move.

Arnie slipped back into the crowd and walked in the opposite direction to the voice. He didn't want to draw attention, not with so many people about. He knew how it would go. One selfie would lead to another twenty and he'd be stuck there for an hour. Arnie usually had a lot of time for people who recognized him, especially when they were polite and civil, but not today. Too much had happened this week, with the attack on Sandy Costello and Tara's shenanigans in Ibiza. He wanted to avoided being asked about it. Most people were well-meaning. They were just naturally nosey. Today, all he wanted was to be a regular guy.

He slipped away unnoticed. As he walked in front of the shops, he saw Gabriel standing outside The Lobster Pot. Arnie came up short, unprepared. He'd come this way without much thought.

Gabriel—Dominic's boyfriend. There was no reason that should change anything between them. *Should it?*

"Hey, man, how's it going?" he asked cheerfully.

Gabriel turned, seemingly surprised. "Arnie. Good to see you. I thought you might have left town."

He didn't go in for a hug, given how uncomfortable their last one had been. "No, I've been lying low, that's all. I couldn't miss today though. Are you kidding? This is our childhood right here."

Gabriel smiled. "I know. Fair day holds a lot of memories, right? It was always one of the highlights of summer growing up. It didn't matter how bad the weather got, we always enjoyed ourselves."

"I've got a bonus now. Being able to relive it all over again through AJ. He's so excited, just like we used to be. I know I'll get some peace tonight 'cause he's going to be so exhausted."

"Where is he? With your mam?"

"No. Sophie took him out for a boat trip."

"Cool. So, what are you doing now?"

"Nothing really. Just wandering. I thought I might stop for a drink soon."

Gabriel put a hand on his arm. "Come on inside. Have one with me. We're in that lull between afternoon service and evening."

"Thanks. I'd love to."

The restaurant was about a third full when they entered as visitors enjoyed a late seafood lunch. Gabriel told Arnie to take a seat in one of the neat leather booths in the bar. As well as serving some of the best seafood for miles, The Lobster Pot also had a smart cocktail bar overlooking the marina.

Arnie settled in a corner booth, glad Gabriel had asked him in. Something had been missing when they had seen each other earlier in the week, as though the old spark of friendship had gone out. Maybe he'd imagined it, or Gabriel had something else on his mind at the time. At least now they would get a second chance.

Gabriel returned a few moments later with champagne served in two long, narrow tulip glasses.

"What's all this about?" Arnie asked. "A beer would have done."

"I feel like being extravagant. It's fair day, after all." He slipped into the booth beside him. "Cheers."

"Cheers."

They clinked glasses and smiled. Like the best of friends, Arnie found it easy to slip back into Gabriel's company.

"I didn't notice the other night, but you've given the bar area a refit," Arnie remarked, pointing out new furnishings, artwork and mirrors behind the bar.

"Little touches," Gabriel said. "Just to keep it fresh. In the winter, we can't rely on the tourist trade, so the cocktails bring in the locals. We have live music too, every weekend. You should come down and check it out. We just do what we can to stay open all year round. It's not always easy in a seasonal town like this."

Arnie nodded, understanding. When he was young and his mother had run a B&B, she'd go for weeks on end without a booking in the winter. It was often the time they would take their family holidays. The summers were too essential to the business for her to take time off then.

"It looks great," Arnie said, sipping the champagne appreciatively. It was delicious and cold. Condensation misted the sides of the glass.

They chatted about work and the success of the fair, about Arnie's career and the upcoming parts he was due to play, about life in the town and how Sandy Costello was still in an induced coma. They spoke about Gabriel's family and AJ's progress at school. They even discussed Tara and the latest batch of photographs to hit the newspapers that morning. There was only one subject they didn't speak about.

Dominic.

Gabriel didn't volunteer any information about his boyfriend and Arnie didn't ask. He didn't begrudge Gabriel a relationship with the sexiest man on the coast. Why should he? Gabriel deserved to be happy. And they seemed perfectly matched — living and working in the town, they had a lot in common. They would look great together too. Dominic, smoldering and dark, and Gabriel, golden and handsome.

He couldn't imagine a better-looking couple.

But Arnie wasn't ready to hear all about that. Not yet. Having met Dominic and read his book, Arnie's crush on him was too strong. He'd get over it, in a day or two, then he'd want to hear about them.

Dominic was Gabriel's man. Arnie had to deal with that.

"I need to get back to work," Gabriel said, draining his glass. "Do you want another?"

"No. I'll leave you to it. I might wander along to The Fisherman's Arms for a drink before I go home. I haven't been in there since last summer. I want to see if anything has changed."

Gabriel laughed. "You know better than that. Nothing has changed in there for fifty years."

"I'd be disappointed if it had. There are some things I never want to change."

They said goodbye at the door. A little of the earlier awkwardness returned. Gabriel told him to come back on Saturday night. "Check out the live music I told you about."

"I will do," he said. "As long as I can get a babysitter."

It was after five when he stepped back onto the waterfront. The crowds had abated somewhat but there was still a huge number of people about. All the stalls were open and looked to be doing great business. He headed along the marina in the direction of The Fisherman's Arms, an old public house that had become an institution in Nyemouth.

Dominic stood in the harbor where the fishing boats were moored, with a collecting bucket and a dynamite smile.

Arnie's heart lurched against his ribs and he stopped at the sight of him, his pulse quickening.

Dominic looked incredible. The navy polo shirt with the official lifeboat logo on the chest suited his tanned skin and displayed the broad lines of his torso and shoulders. His strong forearms appeared golden in the natural light. He wore pale blue shorts turned up to mid-thigh, revealing powerful leg muscles and deliciously hairy calves.

His smile was radiant as a young family walked over to him. The kids took turns to put money in his bucket. He rewarded them all with stickers.

Though he'd read his book and had been thinking about him all week, the sight of Dominic proved that memory and imagination were no match for reality. Dominic was even hotter than he remembered. And his memories were smoking.

Gabriel was a lucky bastard. A *very* lucky bastard.

Arnie considered his options for getting past without being noticed. There were none, other than abandoning his plan to visit the pub and retreating the way he'd come. Should he? *Yes. No. Why do you want to avoid him? Because it's dangerous and I don't trust myself. It's the only way to stop thinking about him.*

The young family moved away, then it was too late. Dominic glanced in his direction and spotted him immediately. Even with his hat and shades, Dominic recognized him and smiled, raising his hand in greeting.

"Hey there."

Oh God, that smile. It was enough to melt him.

"Hi," Arnie said, tightening his stomach and pulling up his chest. He approached, all reservation gone. "You must have been busy today."

"Crazy. This thing weighs a ton," he said, shaking the bucket. "And I've emptied it twice already."

Dominic had caught the sun across his forehead and nose. Beneath the tan, his skin seemed to glow. And so did Arnie. Being close to Dominic sent a surge of heat throughout his body.

"Where have you been all day? I thought I would have seen you around," Dominic said.

You did? The question meant Dominic had been thinking about him too. *And what does that mean? Thinking about me in what way?*

"Oh, I've been around. I took AJ to the fair." He found it difficult to say anything meaningful or funny. Arnie could hold his own on live TV or radio interviews, but face to face with Dominic, he was inexplicably nervous. There was no reason for it.

Other than chemistry.

"Where's the little man now?"

"With my sister. She granted me a few hours of freedom. She must have thought I needed it."

"You look great. People aren't bothering you, are they? There's a lot of folk around today."

"No. Everyone has been polite."

"I'm glad to hear it."

They looked at each other, both smiling, their eyes connected. Neither of them spoke. The chemistry was strong, rendering words unnecessary. Arnie removed his shades and tucked them into the neck of his shirt. Without them, Dominic looked even better, more vivid. The hues of amber and gold in his eyes sparkled in the late afternoon sun.

Arnie glanced away, knowing he shouldn't look at him like that. "I just saw Gabriel," he said.

The sound of his name did nothing to lessen the brightness of Dominic's smile. "Okay," he said.

There was another awkward pause before Arnie added. "We had a drink together. In the restaurant."

Dominic nodded. "You guys went to school together. That's right, isn't it?"

"We did. From nursery to high school."

Dominic's gaze flicked over him uncertainly. "Gabriel's a nice guy."

A nice guy! He's your boyfriend, isn't he? Is that the best you can say about him?

"He's one of the best," Arnie said, watching Dominic carefully for a reaction and failing to see one. It was funny that Gabriel hadn't mentioned him either. Were they keeping it a secret? Playing down their relationship? *Could be.* Gabriel's waters had always run deep. Arnie had to remember that not all gay men were as open as him, especially in small towns like Nyemouth.

It wouldn't be the first time his mother had put about information people would rather not share. He'd shut his mouth on the subject before he embarrassed them both. If Dominic and Gabriel want to be discreet, it was their business and no one else's.

"Where are you heading now?" Dominic asked.

He pointed at the pub behind him. "The Fisherman's Arms," he said with a smile. "I wanted to revisit an old haunt. AJ would be bored to tears in there, so I figured I'd grab a quick drink while I have the time."

Dominic glanced at the pub then back to Arnie. His smile was at full wattage. "Would you mind a little company? The heat out here is killing me. A cool beer in the shade sounds like heaven right now."

"Love to," he answered quickly.

"Great. How about I meet you there in five minutes? Just let me hand this bucket in to the collecting team at the station, then I'll be all yours."

"What are you drinking? I'll get them in."

"A cold pint of lager would be perfect."

Arnie watched him walk away, carrying the heavy bucket of change. His back, his calves, his bum — it was some sight.

It's a dangerous situation, he warned himself. *Dominic is Gabriel's boyfriend. You shouldn't do this.*

There was no harm in it. Two men enjoying a pint together — that was all it was. Dominic was taken and he had every respect for that. They wouldn't do anything other than talk.

Nothing untoward would happen.

Chapter Nine

Dominic moved quickly, ignoring everyone he knew, as he pushed through the lifeboat station and up the stairs to the crew quarters. A long trestle table had been set up in the rear office, where Jacob and two aides were counting the day's takings. Jacob's smile was evidence of how well things had gone. Dominic deposited his bucket with the cluster in the corner that still needed to be counted.

Jacob stacked a neat row of coins and tapped a figure into his calculator.

"Fresh supplies are over there," he said, nodding at a pile of empty buckets.

"Sorry," Dominic said. "I'm done for the day."

"Are things finally dying down out there?"

"No. There's still plenty of folk about. I've got something else to do, that's all."

Jacob pushed his reading glasses to the top of his head and his eyes twinkled.

"Oh, yes. What might that be?"

Dominic laughed. The old man's instincts were razor sharp. "I took your advice," he said. "Don't look so smug about it."

"What advice would that be?" Jacob asked, feigning innocence.

"I'm meeting someone for a drink." He looked at the other people who were counting money. He didn't want to be so obvious as to use Arnie's name in front of them.

Jacob took the hint and grinned. "Then don't keep him waiting. Go on, get out of here. Have a good night."

Dominic dropped into the bathroom before leaving, wanting to check his appearance in the mirror. His nose and forehead were a little pink after an afternoon in the fierce sun. He brushed his fingers through his thick hair, smoothing it down, then ran the cold tap to splash water over his face. He instantly felt better.

A shower would be nice, but there was no time. Arnie was waiting right now. He'd have to take him as he was.

Dominic hurried downstairs, unexpectedly anxious. Why would meeting a guy for a drink have this effect on him? He was a grown man — there was nothing to be nervous about. He could take the boat out in the black of night, into a raging storm, and keep his cool. It was stupid to get worked up over a drink.

Then he realized this had never happened before, being nervy about a guy. Other men had excited him, made him horny for sure, but butterflies in his stomach — that was something new.

Why should Arnie be different?

Because he is.

And Dominic was wasting time when he should be in the pub with him.

As he reached the main entrance, he came to a sudden halt. Gabriel was standing right outside. He groaned inwardly and wondered if he could sneak out another way.

Too late.

"Hey." Gabriel smiled. "I saw you going in and figured you were done for the day. How about coming over for a drink and a bite to eat? You deserve it after a day like this."

Dominic's problem with Gabriel was entirely his own fault. It had been obvious for a while that their no-strings arrangement wasn't as one-sided as it should be, as they'd intended at the start. Gabriel hadn't said as much, but it was clear he wanted more than Dominic was prepared to give, and rather than put him straight, he'd allowed things to drift as they were, hoping Gabriel would get the hint if he cooled off toward him.

It was a coward's solution.

"I've got other plans," he said. "Thanks for the offer. I appreciate it."

Stop trying to play the nice guy, he warned himself. *For fuck's sake, be a man and get it over with. It'll be better in the long run.*

"How about later?" Gabriel said, stepping closer and lowering his voice. "I should be done by ten thirty. Eleven at the latest. I could drop by your place."

Tell him. Gabriel wasn't quick to take a hint.

"No. I don't think so. Look, I don't want to be a dick about this, and I know that's how it'll sound. When we started, we both agreed that this was nothing more than a casual thing. Sex. That was it."

Gabriel's smiled was gone. "I know, but — "

"Let me finish," Dominic said. "Nothing changed for me. I like you a lot, but it was never more than sex. I get the distinct impression you want more than that. Probably a lot more."

"No. You're wrong," Gabriel protested without conviction. "I've never asked for anything from you."

"Okay. I'll accept that. Maybe I'm wrong." A lie. He said it to avoid a scene and hated himself for it. "But we've been seeing more of each other than we ever intended, and if we keep that up, then it's inevitable that deeper feelings will develop."

"Would that be so terrible?" Gabriel's voice was full of hurt. His brown eyes glistened.

"That wasn't the deal," Dominic said softly. "I don't want anything more. I think it's best that we put a stop to all of this. I know it sounds shitty, and I'm sorry. If it's a relationship you're looking for, I'm not the man for you."

"You're wrong," Gabriel said, standing taller, raising his chin. "We are good together. You just don't want to admit it."

"Don't do this."

"Everyone thinks we're a couple. You realize that, don't you?"

"Except we're not."

"We could be. Everyone says we're perfect for each other."

"Who the hell is everyone? Look, Gabriel, I don't care what people think. It's gone far enough. I'm sorry it means more to you than me. I never wanted that. And you told me you didn't either. That's how this started, remember? Because neither of us wanted more."

"Is it because of Arnie?"

"What?"

"I saw you talking to him, not more than ten minutes ago. Don't deny it."

"I'm not. We were standing right there."

"Are you dumping me for him?"

Dominic took a deep breath as frustration built inside him. This was not going well. He could have handled it so much better if he'd had the balls to do it earlier. "I'm not dumping you, because we're not in a relationship. I'm not your boyfriend. I never was."

"You were just fucking me, is that it?"

"Don't do this. We were fucking each other. That's all."

"So I was sufficient until someone better came along."

Dominic had had enough. "I never promised you anything. I made my intentions clear and they haven't changed. If you harboured a hope that it was something meaningful, then I'm sorry. And if you thought I was using you, you could have stopped at any time. I didn't lead you on, Gabriel. Maybe I let the situation continue for longer than it should have. If I did, I'm sorry. It's over. You need to understand that. It has nothing to do with Arnie Walker. It's you and me and no one else."

"Tell yourself the bullshit," Gabriel said, backing away. "Believe it all you want, if it makes you feel better, but things were fine between us until this week, and the only thing that changed was you meeting Arnie. You got a hard-on for him and suddenly you couldn't give a shit about us."

"There is no *us*," he said exasperatedly.

Gabriel was already walking away. "Fuck you, Dominic. You're just a prick." He stomped in the direction of the restaurant.

Strangers stared at Dominic. Their argument had drawn attention. *God damn it.* This was exactly why he avoided relationships. Too much aggravation. Gabriel had been all for their uncomplicated arrangement in the beginning. He'd said he was done with disappointment and being let down. All he'd wanted was sex without the hassle.

Dominic should have known it wouldn't be easy.

He felt like a bastard too. Gabriel was right about one thing — Arnie. Dominic's feelings had changed since meeting him. Things with Gabriel had gone stale. They were seeing too much of each other. It had gotten more complicated than he wanted. Meeting Arnie made him see the situation with fresh eyes.

What did he want from Arnie? He didn't know. Maybe friendship. Maybe nothing. Arnie's personal circumstances and fame gave him cause to think twice. Celebrity and the attention that came with it was not for him. But he couldn't stop thinking about him, imagining them together. He was a developing an infatuation, of a kind which he'd never felt for Gabriel.

Why should he feel guilty about that? He was a free agent. He could do anything he wanted.

Right now, he wanted a drink.

The Fisherman's Arms was a typical old pub. It had one central bar with lots of nooks and annexes shooting off from it. It was very busy when he arrived. They also served food, and it was full of families and couples enjoying an early evening meal after the busy fair.

He found Arnie at a table in the wide bay window, overlooking the marina. He'd taken off his straw hat. After wearing it all afternoon, his thick blond hair was disheveled. It suited him, messing the image of the perfectly groomed actor to present a regular guy.

An *exceptionally handsome* regular guy.

There were two pint glasses on the table in front of him. Arnie only had a quarter left in his. He looked up as Dominic approached, and smiled.

The smile made Dominic forget about all the shit that had just happened.

"Sorry," he said, taking the seat opposite Arnie. "That took a little longer than I expected."

Arnie looked at him warmly. "Don't worry about it. I wasn't going anywhere. Sophie sent a text to say she won't have AJ home until after eight. I intend to enjoy my freedom." He gestured to the pint of lager in front of Dominic. "It's lost its head, but if you're quick, it should still be cold enough."

Dominic picked up the glass and sipped gratefully. His thirst seemed unquenchable, and he downed a third of the drink straight away. "Oh, wow," he gasped. "I needed that a lot more than I thought."

Arnie smiled widely, crinkling his blue eyes. In the natural light of the window, they appeared cobalt. Arnie's looks were breathtaking. Dominic didn't know why that fact took him by surprise each time they met — how drop-dead gorgeous Arnie was. And how his heart beat faster when he saw him.

He reached for the pint again and took another long draught.

"So," he said, pulling it together, "does this place live up to your memories of it?" He raised his eyebrows to indicate the surrounding bar.

Arnie followed his gaze. "Some of the furniture has been reupholstered, and there's a new carpet in the entrance. Other than that, nothing has changed. I'd have been disappointed if it had."

"I don't come in here much," Dominic said. "I can't even remember the last time. Maybe last Guy Fawkes Night when we were out collecting." *I'm rambling.* He didn't know what else to say.

"I doubt I'd be bothered with it that much if I lived here. I think I just appreciate it more because I don't. You miss things like this when you don't have them. Or maybe I'm getting sentimental in my old age."

"Hardly. What are you? Thirty?"

"Thirty-four."

"You don't look it. Whenever thirty-four is supposed to look like. Age means nothing once you're over twenty-five. As long as you've got good health and the motivation to enjoy it."

"How old are you? If you have all this wisdom."

Dominic chuckled. "Thirty-seven, just last month."

"Whatever it is you do, you must tell me your secret."

"It's doing what you love and enjoying life. Too many people don't. Since I came to Nyemouth, all the pieces have fallen perfectly into place."

Arnie finished his drink. Dominic went to the bar to get another two. He touched his forehead while he waited to be served. The skin was hot. Was he blushing? Arnie certainly had some kind of effect on him. Butterflies were dancing in his stomach.

"I finished your book," Arnie said when he returned to the table.

"Which one?" he asked, draining his old glass.

"*Hard to Kill.*"

Arie rested his forearms on the table and leaned forward. Dominic breathed in the smell of him – the scent of his aftershave, the masculine odor of his body. It was heady and intoxicating. He imagined inhaling it fresh off his skin, from the hair on his chest or the intimacy of his groin. Suddenly there was a picture in his mind — Arnie standing above him in a pair of snug white briefs, Dominic pressing his face against the fullness of the cotton.

"That was my first book," he said, snapping his focus back to the moment.

"It doesn't read that way," Arnie said. "It was very accomplished. I've always shied away from the action genre. I imagined they'd be too complicated to follow and dense with technology and info dumps. Your book wasn't like that. Despite everything that was going on, all the characters and double crosses, it was an easy read."

"Thank you. That's one of the best things a writer can hear. No one wants to be told they a wrote a difficult read, or that it was a struggle to follow."

"I'm not just saying it to flatter you. I mean it. My dad has given me another one to read. *Die Trying*."

"I believe you," he said, laughing. "And thank you again. When my next one comes out, I'll ask you to give a quote for the cover."

Arnie sipped his beer, licked foam from his top lip then said, "You used a pen name, but the author bio at the back, that sounds true. You were in the Royal Marines and Special Boat Service, right?"

"Yes, that's all true. It's only the pen name that's made up."

"Is that because of the Official Secrets Act?"

"No," he said, bemused. "That would only come into play if I wanted to write a memoir. Because my books are all fiction, it doesn't matter. I decided to use a pen name for privacy. I would probably sell more copies if I put a photo on the cover and went on a publicity tour, signing books and giving readings, that kind of thing."

"Why don't you? If it means selling more."

"I don't want to, and I don't need to. The books have done all right. Well enough for them to publish more. I'm happy to be an unknown author."

"I understand that." Arnie looked straight into his eyes, without embarrassment, seemingly without fear of intimacy. "How long were you in the services?"

"Fourteen years in all. I joined at eighteen rather than go to university. It was the making of me, though I suppose it was already in my blood. My father was in the RAF and we moved around a lot when I was young. I loved everything about the life. The service, the discipline, the honour and the travel. The danger and excitement. I've always been somewhat of an adrenaline junkie and the marines was perfectly suited to that. That's why I applied to the Boat Service when I was twenty-six, to chase a bigger high."

"Why give it up when you loved it so much?"

He shrugged. "Everything has its time, I suppose. I was in my early thirties and ready for something different. All I'd ever known were the services. I wanted something…normal. A house, a dog, a place to call home at last."

"And you came here?"

"I don't know why I chose this town over any other. I wanted space, so a city was out of the question. I wanted a project, and the house was pretty run down when I bought it, so the redevelopment kept me busy. And there was the lifeboat, which satisfied my love of the sea and my need for action."

Talking to Arnie was easy. Dominic opened up to him in ways he wouldn't have thought possible. The only other person he could communicate with like this was Jacob, and they had been friends for years.

"You sound like superman," Arnie said in a good-natured way. "Your books, the lifeboat, renovating your own house. There doesn't appear to be anything you can't turn your hand to."

"I'm not much of a cook," he said with a laugh. "What about you? I feel like I've done all the talking. Tell me something about you."

Arnie sighed. "I hate talking about myself. Whenever I have a movie or a show to promote, I end up doing a long round of press and answer the same old questions. Most of my answers are pre-rehearsed."

"So, tell me something real. Not about Arnie the actor. I want to know about the man and the father."

"That's even harder to do."

"Okay. Tell me what you hate. What pisses you off? I mean really drives you mad."

He took another sip of beer, seeming to give it some thought. "I can't stand rudeness and unprofessionalism. Even worse, when those things go together. Actors or directors who treat people on the crew like shit, like they're nothing. Everyone had a job to do and they're all equally important to a production. I hate it when people don't get that."

"What else?"

"Buffets," he said with a laugh. "I can't stand buffets."

"What's wrong with them?"

Arnie screwed up his face. "Everything. Standing in line, the indecision, piling up a plate with crap you really don't want to eat. There's so much waste."

Dominic laughed. "I don't think I agree, but I can see where you're coming from. Sort of. Now tell me about something you do like."

"Okay," Arnie said, getting into it. "I love Italian food. Greek too. Especially their lamb dishes. I like red wine and vodka cocktails."

"We'll have to differ there. I hate red wine. I don't much like wine at all. But I'm with you on the food. I love Greek and Italian cooking."

"Wine goes perfectly with that kind of food. A nice bottle of red with a slow-cooked piece of lamb or beef. I can't imagine anything better."

Arnie looked him straight in the eyes. His pupils were large and dilated. Dominic was suddenly emboldened. What was he waiting for? There might never be another chance like this one.

"Would you like to go out with me?" The words came freely from his mouth. "If you like that kind of food, we've got some great restaurants all along the coast. I'd love to check them out. Maybe you can even convert me about the wine."

Arnie's broad smile grew straight and serious. The silence as he looked across the table was interminable. *Fuck. I've read the signals completely wrong. He isn't interested in me at all. Why would he be?*

Arnie's eyes were hard to read. "What about Gabriel?"

Dominic swallowed before answering. "What about him?"

"I thought you two were an item," Arnie said, tilting his head to one side.

"An item? Why? Did he tell you we were?"

"No. Actually, he didn't. It was my mother who did."

Dominic let out a long breath. "That's the downside of living in a small town. Everyone thinks they know what's going on."

Arnie leaned closer. "Sorry. I took her at her word. Does that mean you're not seeing him?"

Damn it! What should he do now? Lie? No, that was not the way forward. He liked Arnie too much to lie to him now. It could fuck up any chance he might have.

"We had a thing," he said, struggling for a way to describe the situation that didn't sound completely sleazy. "I think your mother, and a few other people, would like it to be a lot more than that, but the truth is, it isn't. It never was."

"I don't understand. Are you seeing him or not?"

"There's no nice way of putting this, so I'll just say it. We were fuck buddies."

Arnie's eyebrows shot up and he sat back in his seat.

"Sorry," Dominic continued, watching his chances slip away. "That's all it ever was. Just two guys helping each other out. We didn't go on dates or buy each other presents. It was just sex. We can't have been as discreet as I thought we were if people are talking, but that's all that we were, friends with benefits."

Arnie smiled and shook his head. His shock and disappointment were obvious. "It's okay. You don't have to explain."

"I want to. And I'm not asking you out because I expect the same from you. There's nothing between me and Gabriel. I don't want the idea to colour your judgement of me. I want to go out with you because I'm interested in you. I feel something for you. I don't know what it is, but I haven't stopped thinking about you since we met last Sunday." Now his mouth was running wild on him, but he couldn't stop. Maybe

Arnie wasn't interested. Maybe he didn't fancy him. He could handle that. He just didn't want to be rejected over some misunderstanding with Gabriel.

Arnie leaned forward again. "I like you too," he said quietly. "A lot. It's just that there's so much going on in my life right now. I brought AJ here to give him some stability, and I don't think the time is right for me to start seeing someone. Not when his mother is splashed all over the media."

Dominic would not give in that easily. "I get that, and I'm willing to take things as quietly and as slowly as you want them. Let me take you out somewhere, this week, next week, I don't care when—just give me something to hope for."

Arnie looked at him carefully, seemingly undecided.

"If the thing about Gabriel bothers you, why not talk to him first?" Dominic pressed. "He might not be thrilled at the idea, but I know you're old friends. I don't think he'd lie to you."

"That might be an awkward conversation," Arnie said with a hint of amusement. "*Would you be okay if I went to dinner with your fuck buddy? As long you're done with him, of course.*"

"I'll speak to him on your behalf," he said.

"You sure are keen," Arnie said, breaking into a broad grin. "All right. I'll take a chance on you."

"You will?" His soul rose up.

"Yes."

"When?"

"Let's say this week sometime. I don't have your freedom. I'll need to talk someone into babysitting. I'll let you know tomorrow when I get something arranged."

"Any time you like. I don't have any other plans, and if I did, I'd change them."

Dominic's smile was uncontrollable. Today had been a triumph in all sorts of ways, and now it had just got better.

Chapter Ten

Arnie crossed the bridge to the south side of the river and began the ascent to Cliff House. A beautiful day had given way to a perfect evening. The cloudless sky had deepened in color to a rich blue. It would soon be twilight. It was balmy too, without a breath of wind from the sea to cool the still heat.

Arnie's mood was as clear as the sky after spending time with Dominic. The chemistry between them affected him more deeply than the alcohol they had drunk. His steps were light as he followed the steep path up the cliff. His body tingled from the top of his scalp to his toes. Feathery fingers of electricity skittered down his spine. He did not feel like a thirty-four-year-old man, more like fourteen. Only better. Arnie laughed.

It was ridiculous.

He'd never experienced these emotions before, not even when he was young. He'd been too busy building a career and hiding his feelings to get excited about boys.

And Dominic was exciting. No one who spent more than a minute with him could deny that. It was more than his stunning looks or the amazing things he'd done with his life. It was his charm and charisma — they seemed unlimited and radiated from him.

Now they were going on a date. Arnie smiled just thinking about it. *A date.*

At my age. How old-fashioned. How exciting.

Part of him remained cautious. There was no doubt that he'd get a babysitter for AJ. His parents would watch him any time he asked. Sophie too. The childcare story was a ruse, giving him an excuse to take things slowly. He would call Dominic tomorrow after sleeping on the idea.

There was little chance of changing his mind, but he had to think about more than himself. AJ was his top priority. Arnie had no intention of putting his personal life on hold until AJ went off to college, but this was a strange time for both of them. He'd brought his son to Nyemouth so they could spend the summer together. Not to hook up with some random guy after just one week.

Dominic was no random guy, that was true. He was intelligent, brave, charming, and Arnie's parents were already in awe of him. Only Arnie couldn't afford to take it at face value. He'd met Dominic three times, all inside a week. And his parents didn't really know him as well as they thought they did. His mother was happy to spread the rumor that Dominic and Gabriel were in a relationship, when in fact they were just friends with benefits.

And what about that? Should he talk to Gabriel before agreeing to this date? Check he wasn't stepping on anyone's toes. That would not be an easy conversation. They might be lifelong friends, but Arnie and Gabriel had never been able to talk about intimate stuff. Their careers, their hobbies, music and movies were all fair game, but emotions and sex had always been taboo. There had been a handful of times in the past when he'd offered some personal insight during one of their conversations. Without exception, Gabriel had shut it down and changed the subject.

Arnie had always figured he wasn't comfortable and left things alone.

So how would he broach this matter?

Hey, I hear you've been fucking Dominic. Anything you want to tell me before I take a ride?

Gabriel would have a fit.

The fact that he had a casual sex life was a major surprise in itself. Arnie believed his unwillingness to talk about sex meant he had no interest in it. Yet here he was, the fuck buddy of the hottest man in town.

It proves you never really know someone.

And was even more reason to be careful.

He didn't know Dominic at all. Looks and first impressions weren't everything. They could go on a date and spend time getting to know each other better, but he would have to be sure of him before allowing it to go any further. The stability of his family was at stake, and there was no way he'd risk that for a hot guy with a juicy arse.

Arnie paused three-quarters of the way home. He'd reached the foot of the steps that would take him to the top of the cliff. He stopped for a moment to admire the view of the town below. The river and the water of the marina were perfectly still, like a topaz mirror. On Sunday evening, the harbor was full, with most of the fishing boats home from the sea. This time tomorrow there would only be a fraction of the fleet down there.

Most of the visitors had left now they had packed away the fair, though the waterfront still looked busy, with The Lobster Pot and various takeaway outlets doing great business.

Not for the first time, a wave of nostalgia for the town hit Arnie. He'd always known a part of his soul lingered in Nyemouth. He'd traveled around the world, but none of the places he'd visited or worked influenced him like this. New York, Hollywood, Rome, Sydney, the south coasts of Italy and Greece — he loved them, but not as much as Nyemouth.

Now, more than ever, this felt like home.

His gaze moved high above the town, to South Bank Terrace, just about opposite from where he stood — one of the oldest streets in Nyemouth. He wondered which of the sandstone houses belonged to Dominic. Jacob Chisholm owned the second from the end nearest the cliff. He'd lived there all of Arnie's life. Dominic had said Jacob was his neighbor. That could mean anything. It didn't have to be the house next door. Even from here, on the other side of the valley, he could see how Dominic had fallen in love with the place. Perched above the river, with panoramic views of the sea and shore, South Bank Terrace wasn't just prime real estate for Nyemouth, but this whole area of the North East coast.

He turned and headed up the steps. Sophie would have AJ home soon. The little man would be worn out after a long day and Arnie wanted him in bed by nine.

There was still no breeze, even at the top of the cliff, but the air was cool and salty. Arnie filled his lungs and smiled as he walked along the side of the road toward the house.

I could get used to living here again. It was a tempting thought, but unrealistic. As idyllic as Nyemouth was, it was too removed from his work opportunities.

Approaching the house, Arnie was pleased to see there were no cars parked out front. No vehicles in any direction. There had been no reporters for three days. It looked like the heat might be off. He hoped so.

As he came to the front gate of Cliff House, he was distracted, looking forward to the evening ahead, putting AJ to bed and maybe watching TV before turning in early himself. He didn't notice a sudden movement by the tree to the right of the house. Not at first. Just a dark blur at the edge of his vision.

He turned his head quickly and saw — thought he saw — a figure run from the base of the tree around the far side of the house.

Suddenly he was alert.

A dark figure, like the one last Sunday on the cliff. Sandy Costello's attacker. No. He was mistaken. It couldn't be.

Why not? The police had yet to arrest anyone for the incident. The attacker was still at large.

And here now?

It was a waste of time to speculate. Arnie hurried toward the corner where the figure had disappeared, more angry than afraid. He had no weapon and there was nothing in front of the house he could improvise with. He didn't care. He'd had extensive fight training for several of his films so he knew how to take care of himself. And at six-foot-four, if anyone tried to take him on, it would be their loss.

No fucking mercy.

He turned the corner. The long exterior wall of the house and garden ran in a straight line ahead, reflecting golden light in the evening sun. To the right was a patch of lilac, too short to conceal someone, and in the distance a wooded area of black poplar trees. If the figure tried to make for them, he would see them.

Meaning only one thing. They had gone behind the house.

Moving fast, keeping to the side, Arnie followed. The garden wall was too high for anyone to scramble over. There was no ivy or nearby trees to aid anyone in an attempt. The woods were nearer here. From the cover of the wall, the stranger could have made it to the dark protection of the poplars without being seen.

Arnie scanned the dense tree line and saw no one. It was useless. The shadows were so deep, a figure dressed in black would become invisible just a yard or two inside.

God damn. He doubted himself. Had he really seen anyone at all? The movement had been so fast, just a glimpse from the corner of his eye. He'd had a few drinks in town and hadn't been completely alert when he'd seen it.

Bullshit. Three drinks did not affect him that much, and he'd had his eyes tested five weeks ago. He needed glasses to read, but his distance and peripheral sight were near perfect. It had been no trick of the light or imagination. What he'd seen was real.

Arnie walked the full perimeter of the house. Careful. Alert. He looked and listened, detecting nothing. The background noise was barely perceptible on such a still evening — he couldn't even hear the waves on the beach. Returning to the front gate, it was clear he was alone.

The figure he'd seen must have made off into the woods under the cover of the back wall. It was the only possible conclusion. Arnie was more concerned about who he had seen than where they'd gone.

It could have been a journalist or photographer. Except, from experience, he knew they were more likely to rush toward their target, camera or microphone raised, than run away from them. Which left him with the grim possibility that the person who'd thrown Sandy Costello from the cliff had sought the only witnesses to the crime.

* * * *

The following morning, Arnie sat at the desk in the ground floor office. Behind him, Police Community Support Officer Narinder Shah looked over his shoulder as he cued up the CCTV footage.

"I came home around a quarter to eight," he explained, "which is when I saw them. I worked backward through the recording until I found this."

The camera was focused on the front of the house, covering the road and the tree to the side. At eight minutes past six on the display clock, a figure dressed entirely in black — jeans, hoodie, balaclava — came into shot around the side wall. Moving with stealth, they approached the front gate and stared thought the iron bars. They spent the next six minutes looking at the house as though assessing it. Peering through the courtyard, gazing at the upstairs windows. There was something terrible about the balaclava-clad face, like a masked maniac in a horror film.

After several minutes, the figure moved over to the tree and, with what appeared to be minimal effort, climbed up into the branches.

"He sits there for almost an hour and a half," Arnie said, speeding through the footage until the moment he came home.

As Arnie approached the gate, the figure leapt out of the tree with the agility of a cat and hurried down the side of the house and out of sight.

"If he hadn't moved, I would never have known he was there," Arnie said.

"Do you pick him up on any of the other cameras?" PSCO Shah asked.

"No. The ones on the back only cover the garden area and courtyard. They don't extend over the wall."

"Pity," she said. "You think he went into the woods?"

"It's the only place he could have gone. I wasn't going to chase in after him to find out. There's nowhere else to hide back there."

"Are you aware of any attempt to gain entry to the house?"

"No. The alarm system is first rate. There are sensors all over the place. I checked the panel when I came in and none of the zones had been triggered."

"Does the system have a panic alarm?"

"Yes."

"Good. If you're ever in the house and feel in danger, use it."

She asked to watch the footage through again. Arnie took it back.

"Have you seen this person before last night?" she asked.

"Around the house, no, but seen them before, certainly. I'm sure it's the person who attacked Sandy Costello."

"What makes you so sure?"

As the stranger reappeared on the screen, Arnie paused the image. "The clothes for one. They're identical. What are the chances of two people dressing head to toe in black with a balaclava in the middle of summer? In broad daylight. Slight at best, don't you think? Not just that, though – the height and build are the same too. And it can't be a coincidence that the week after I witnessed an assault, someone who fits the attacker's description cases out my home."

"Have you received any threats?"

"Not directly. I don't know about social media, though. I have accounts but I don't monitor them. But people write all sorts of crap online. It doesn't mean they intend to go through with the things they say."

The young officer scribbled in her notebook. "I'll take a look at your accounts just the same. You're right, I don't think this person" – she pointed at the still image on screen – "is going to announce themselves, but we can't rule it out. Can I get a copy of this footage?"

He handed her a flash drive. "I've already downloaded it for you."

"Good. This will do for now, but I'd like your permission to download all the footage from the last week. That way we can check through it, just in case this wasn't their first visit."

"Sure. Anything you want. Take it all."

She smiled reassuringly. "As you say, the house has a first-rate security system, but I'm going to arrange for a marker on this address. That means a rapid response.

If you see anything that worries you, or you have any concerns, call 9-9-9, and a police unit will be here straight away. We'll also increase the frequency of drive-by checks on this road. There's just you and your son living here at the moment. Is that right?"

"Yes. But AJ doesn't know about this." He pointed at the monitor. "I don't want to frighten him."

"I understand. It might be a good idea if you could get someone to stay with you for a while. And take every precaution. Keep the doors locked, even when you're home. Set the alarm when you go to bed."

"I do all those things anyway," he said. "I'm hyper vigilant. An over-enthusiastic fan once got onto a film set and I found her in my bed when I returned to my trailer. Ever since then, I've been super-conscious of security."

"That's good, but you need to be extra vigilant right now. Don't take any chances. No risks. Drive, don't walk, when you go into town. Don't travel alone. Stay with a group of people if you can."

Arnie looked at her sideways. "Is there something you're not telling me? Do you know more about this than I do?"

"No," she said, deadly serious. "This is something out of the ordinary for all of us. We just don't get incidents like it in Nyemouth. We've had murders for sure, but they're always domestics, or drug or alcohol related. And guys at the weekend who have too much to drink and beat the hell out of each other. But what happened last weekend was a first. And it pains me to say, we're no further forward or close to making an arrest. You have a lovely son. I just want you to take care of him."

"I always do."

She nodded. "This will help too." She held up the flash drive. "I'm sure the inspector will authorize a search of the woods once she's seen it. I don't believe for a minute they're still out there, but they may have left something behind to help us identify them."

As he listened to her speak, he wondered just how safe Nyemouth was for AJ. This nutcase had very likely found out where they were living, and the police were saying they couldn't guarantee their protection.

Was it really worth seeing out the summer here after everything that had happened?

Maybe, he thought, *it's time to pack up and return to London.*

Nyemouth no longer felt like home.

Chapter Eleven

Dominic didn't hear from Arnie at all on Monday or Tuesday, despite sending him a couple of friendly text messages. He couldn't understand the silent treatment. It had seemed to go so well on Sunday — they'd done everything but set a date and time for going out together. Then nothing. What had happened to switch Arnie from hot to cold?

Gabriel? He appeared an obvious answer, and hardly a surprise if it turned Arnie off. Few guys would be pleased to learn they were getting an old friend's sloppy seconds. Without being callous, it was no easy thing convincing Arnie that Gabriel meant nothing to him. He wondered if they'd spoken to each other, if Gabriel had warned Arnie to back off.

Funny how Gabriel had only mentioned Arnie once, the last time they'd slept together. Nothing he'd said convinced Dominic they were lifelong friends. Quite the opposite. Gabriel was dismissive of Arnie, bitchy even.

But he'd certainly been pissed off when they had spoken on Sunday. Angry enough to stick the knife in? He hoped not, but the idea, once in his mind, wouldn't quit. How well did he know Gabriel, anyway? He could be capable of anything. He was an occasional bedfellow. Dominic's knowledge of him went no deeper than that. Maybe Gabriel wouldn't think twice about sabotaging things between him and Arnie.

Only there isn't anything to sabotage. Yet.

His fears were proved unfounded on Wednesday when Jacob brought Brandy back from his early morning walk into town.

"Have you heard about Arnie?" Jacob asked, standing by the kitchen door.

"No," he said, failing hide his concern.

"It seems the clifftop attacker paid him a visit."

"What?" The alarm was completely genuine. "Is he all right? When did this happen?"

"Sunday night. After the fair. He's okay, I think. A bit spooked. Who wouldn't be? Apparently, they've got footage of this man on CCTV."

"Do they know who it is? Have they picked him up?"

"No. He was in disguise. Kept his face covered."

"Shit." No wonder Arnie had been indifferent to his text messages. He had much bigger problems than romance. "Is Arnie all right? Have they have threatened him?"

"No. By the sound of things, this person may have been casing the house. He ran up to the woods when Arnie returned and startled him. As you can imagine, it gave him a fright, especially when he's got the boy at home. From what I hear, he's thinking about cutting their holiday short and heading back to London. Can't say I'd blame him if they did."

"No," Dominic said. "Neither would I."

Safety had to be the priority, especially with a young son, but the idea of Arnie leaving town, of not seeing him again, gripped Dominic somewhere deep inside, twisting his guts and squeezing hard. His breathing became shallow as panic set in.

When Jacob left, he tried to work. It was no good. He couldn't concentrate on his characters or plot or the world he was trying to create. All he could think about was Arnie. His emotions were a confusion of fear, loss, anger and desperation. The attacker — the potential killer — had tracked him down, had found out where he was living. What kind of sick fucker would do that?

The kind that attacks random strangers.

What the hell was their intention now?

Who knows what goes on in a mind like that?

Dominic could take no more. He picked up the phone.

Arnie answered straight away. "Hi."

Hearing his voice was a relief. Until that moment, Dominic hadn't known how much he wanted to hear it. "Are you okay? I heard what happened."

"Yes. Sorry I didn't call you. It's been intense."

"Don't worry about me. I'm just happy to know you're all right."

There was a second of hesitation until Arnie said, "I'm glad you called. I'd love to see you."

"Anytime."

Another pause. "Can you come over? Now?"

He didn't have to think about his answer. "I'll be there in twenty minutes."

* * * *

Dominic had passed Cliff House countless times in the last five years, by foot and car. He'd never given it much thought. It was one of those places that had always been there. The kind of place local people paid no attention to, while tourists paused to admire its historic beauty.

When he pressed the intercom, the electric gate swung softly open and he pulled through into the private car park. The gate closed behind him. He couldn't think of a safer, more secure place in the whole town, and yet the thought of Arnie and AJ alone up here, so far from their closest neighbor, was an uneasy one.

Arnie appeared from around the back of the house, dressed in a nautical-looking blue-and-white-striped T-shirt with pale blue shorts that showed off his tanned, muscular limbs.

As Dominic approached him to say hello, Arnie flung his arms around him and pulled him into a firm embrace. Dominic accepted the contact willingly, wrapping his own arms around Arnie's back and shoulders. They stayed like that, not moving, the sides of their heads touching.

"Thanks for coming," Arnie murmured. "It's so good to see you."

"I would have come sooner. As soon as I heard the news, I called."

"You're here now—that's what matters most. This place has been crazy. The police, my parents, my sister. This morning is the first time I've had to myself all week."

"Where is everyone now?"

"My folks have taken AJ and his cousins out for the day. They've driven up to Berwick. They want me to go with them, but I just needed a few hours to myself. At least I thought I did until you called."

They stood for a few moments longer. Holding Arnie felt so good. Not in a sexual way, though the attraction Dominic felt for him was undeniable. It was more than that, better. There was nothing uncomfortable about the embrace. The opposite was true. Even though Arnie was a few inches taller than him and Dominic had to stretch to make contact, it was perfect.

"Let's go inside," Arnie said at last.

Dominic walked at his side, around the back of the house, to a patio where French doors led to an open-plan kitchen and living area. He lingered for a moment on the terrace, checking out the garden and the height of the wall that surrounded it. Though it would not be easy to climb, a seasoned criminal would have no trouble getting over. Once they did, there were a lot of potential hiding places in the well-established shrubbery and foliage of the garden.

Cliff House was not as safe as his first impression had suggested.

The interior was a surprise. Dominic expected it to have been completely modernized, in the way of most redeveloped old properties. Whoever had been responsible for the overhaul of the house had done so with complete sympathy for the age and style of the original, with lots of natural wood and traditional features. Dominic had done most of the work on his own house himself, besides a couple of electrical jobs he'd had to contract out. It was clear to his experienced eye that they had done the refurbishment of this place to the highest standards.

And although it was only a rental, the house seemed perfectly suited to Arnie. It was handsome, smart, old-fashioned and current all at once.

He liked it a lot.

Dominic closed and locked the French windows behind them.

"That's okay," Arnie said. "You can leave them open."

Dominic shook his head in admonishment. "Security, remember. Take nothing for granted."

Arnie nodded grimly. "You'd think the message would have sunk in by now, huh?"

"Don't ever be too careful. Your circumstances right now, they demand utmost caution."

"Duly noted." He laughed softly and smacked his own wrist. "How about a drink? I've got juice, lemonade. Beer and wine if you want something stronger."

"A Diet Coke would be nice, if you have it. Otherwise water is fine."

Arnie took two large glasses from one of the cupboards and drew ice from the refrigerator. Dominic perched on a chair at the end of the breakfast bar and watched him as he opened a two-liter bottle of Diet Coke and poured. He loved looking at him and watching the way he moved. Arnie had kicked off his sandals at the door and walked around the kitchen in bare feet, reminding Dominic of a sexy deckhand in his shorts and T-shirt combo. His skin was darker than when they'd first met, its golden tones evidence of the outstanding weather they'd enjoyed this last week.

Even the pale blond hairs on his legs seemed to have caught the sun.

It was Arnie's eyes that betrayed the strain he was under. There was a slight puffiness in the skin beneath them, and dark shadows evidenced a clear lack of sleep.

He approached the counter with their drinks and sat on the end, at an angle to Dominic.

"Thanks," Dominic said, taking a sip, watching all the while.

"Thanks again for coming," Arnie said. "You have no idea how much it means to me, seeing you today." He sighed. "On Monday morning, I was all set to pack our things and head back to London. I'd had enough. It seems this fucker wants to play games. Dangerous games."

"No one would blame you if you left," Dominic said. "Most folk would be gone by now. Especially with a child in the house."

"That's it. Even now that I've decided to stay a little longer, I'll suddenly catch myself and wonder what the hell I'm playing at. I can't take chances with my son. The safest thing to do is get out. But then I get angry. Nyemouth is also my home. More so than anywhere else, and I won't be driven away by some random nutcase. I want AJ to know his grandparents, his aunt and his cousins. He's got lots of friends in London, but it's not the same as family. Tara's side don't bother with him, so it's doubly important that he has a connection here. If we leave now, it might damage that forever."

As he spoke, Dominic saw a vulnerability to Arnie that was all new. He was a conflicted man, struggling to give his son the love and family he deserved while weighing up their safety. Dominic had no attachment to his own family. His mother was still alive. His brothers lived abroad. He had a minor interest in their lives and occasionally caught up on what they were doing via social media, but there was no real love there. Not like the love Arnie had for his son and his parents. Dominic's indifference to his family only made him appreciate what Arnie was trying to do even more.

"What have the police done?" he asked.

"Someone came the other day and downloaded the CCTV footage for the whole of last week. They want to check for any earlier visits from the stalker. That's what I've started calling him — the stalker."

"It fits. That's what he is. Though 'sick bastard' works too."

"For sure. Anyway, I haven't heard whether they've found anything. There are meant to be frequent police patrols going past the house. If there are, I haven't spotted them, but then again, I haven't been glued to the window watching for them either. I'm trying to keep things as normal as possible for AJ's sake. That's the main reason I didn't want to go with them today. I needed some time away from him, just to drop the mask of normality for a couple of hours."

Dominic put his hand on Arnie's forearm. "What can I do?"

For a moment Arnie looked overwhelmed by the question and his eyes glistened with moisture. "Just this," he said at last. "Your being here is a massive help."

"I want to do more," he said. "If the police won't look after your security, let me. I can be a night watchman. I'll be awake while the two of you sleep. Check the perimeter, watch the cameras. If that crazy bastard is dumb enough to drop by again, he'll be sorry to find me home."

"I'm sure he would. But you can't do that."

"I mean it. It's not right, the police leaving you here without protection."

"They advised me not to be alone."

"See. Then let me stay. You'll never find a better bodyguard. Or more qualified," he added with a cheeky grin to lighten the mood.

Arnie laughed. "I appreciate it, but I can't let you put yourself out like that. Besides, my parents have offered to move in too. I told them no."

"Your dad is a great guy, but at his age, I think you'll be the one protecting him."

Arnie moved his hand and put it on top of Dominic's. "Thank you, but no thanks."

"If you change your mind, the offer stands."

"I won't," Arnie said. "But there is one thing I do want from you."

Before Dominic could question what, Arnie came in for a kiss, pressing his lips against Dominic's. The move was unexpected and completely wanted. His wide lips covered Dominic's, and when his tongue moved into his mouth, Dominic yielded, accepting it willingly. All of his senses became heightened as he experienced Arnie with every part of his body. He wrapped his hand around the back of Arnie's head, feeling the softness of his hair, and drew him deeper into the kiss. Their lips were silky together, while the stubble on their faces rasped as they rubbed against each other. Arnie smelled fresh and clean, with a slight spicy essence coming from his cologne.

"I needed that," Arnie said, breaking the contact, his forehead pressed against Dominic's. "You have no idea how badly."

Dominic breathed heavily, his hand still on the back of Arnie's head. "You'd better believe I do."

They rose to their feet, coming together, their arms wrapped around each other. The kisses were deeper now, full of passion. Dominic couldn't believe the height of arousal Arnie took him to. He held him and noted the breadth and strength of his body. He put his hands on Arnie's hips, drawing him tight, feeling the hot swelling in his shorts. Arnie was a big man, and everything appeared to be in perfect proportion.

Dominic wondered whether he could take it and batted away the concern in an instant. He would take it whatever.

Arnie grabbed the bottom of Dominic's polo shirt and hauled it up. He raised his arms, allowing Arnie to strip him. Arnie looked down at him appraisingly.

"Wow," he said, running his hand over Dominic's muscular chest, snaking his fingers through the dark hair. "You're even hotter than I imagined."

Dominic shuddered as Arnie drew a circle around his left nipple. Both nipples were hard. He gently tweaked the swollen nub and tugged. Dominic gasped in pleasure. Then Arnie's hands were at the waist of his shorts, unfastening his belt.

"I want to see all of you," Arnie said.

Dominic gave no resistance. Arnie undid his fly and his shorts fell to his ankles. Dominic kicked off his shoes and stepped out of the shorts. Arnie ran his hands along Dominic's torso, across the furry plane of his belly, around his hips, to his back, down to this arse. He took his butt in a two-handed grip and squeezed the firm muscle.

"I wanted to grab your arse the first time I saw you," Arnie said, brushing his lips across Dominic's face.

"Be my guest," he said breathlessly. "Do whatever you want."

Arnie grasped and kneaded. Dominic raised onto his toes, giving him freer access. He felt the heat of Arnie's bare hand slipping down the rear of his boxer-briefs, cupping his cheeks, his fingertips curling into the crack. The pressure of Arnie's erection against his belly was immense.

Arnie shoved Dominic's underwear to the floor. He stepped out of them and kicked them away. Now he was naked, while Arnie remained fully clothed. Arnie stepped back to admire his body.

"Perfect," he said, stroking the length of Dominic's hard cock with a light hand, going all the way down the shaft to cup his smooth balls.

Dominic had no issues with body hair — he liked men to be men — but it required a degree of grooming in the groin. He kept his pubes neatly trimmed and scrotum smooth. Arnie held the hairless sac in the palm of his hand and lifted his balls, exploring with tenderness. His cock seemed harder than ever, the head extending through his foreskin. Arnie drew his fingers back along the shaft before taking it in a firm grip. He squeezed. Dominic juddered and watched clear fluid leak from the end of his cock.

He grabbed Arnie's wrist. "You need to take it easy," he said. "You've got me too turned on."

Arnie silenced him with a kiss, returning both hands to his arse. He spread Dominic's cheeks. Dominic shuddered afresh as Arnie ran his fingertip along the seam and gently circled his hole.

"Do you bottom?" Arnie asked, still kissing him.

"For the right guy," Dominic replied, pressing his body against the bulge in Arnie's shorts. "And you are the right guy."

Arnie grinned. "Give me a minute to get a condom."

"There's one in my wallet. In my shorts."

Dominic retrieved the rubber and a sachet of lube and allowed Arnie to lead him naked to the wooden dining table. He hitched his butt onto the edge of the table and lay back, pulling his thighs into his chest, high and wide. Dominic hadn't been lying. He almost never offered himself up like this, and certainly not on the first encounter. With Arnie, he wanted to tear up the rule book. To cast aside every macho inhibition.

He wanted to be filled by Arnie.

Dominic wanted to be fucked.

Arnie pulled off his T-shirt. Looking up, Dominic did a quick appraisal of his body. His chest and torso were toned, but not overly so. His belly was flat and sexy, without the definition of a six-pack. The perfect package was covered in honey-colored hair.

Arnie slipped off his shorts and briefs.

"Oh my God," Dominic said, catching sight of his big, uncut cock. "That's huge."

"Still want to go through with this?" Arnie said, the condom wrapper unopened his hand.

"Fuck yes. Get it in me."

Arnie put on the rubber and coated the full length in lube. He emptied the remainder of the sachet into Dominic's crack and fingered it into his hole. Dominic was tight. He drew a deep breath and willed his body to relax.

You can do this. You'd better fucking do this.

His head shot up from the table as Arnie pushed against the resistance of his opening.

"Okay?" Arnie asked, pausing.

Dominic breathed deeply and gripped the edge of the table. He nodded. "Keep going."

He felt himself stretch, opening wider and wider, being filled in a way that seemed impossible. Arnie took his time, letting him adjust before pushing more of his cock inside.

Fuck, that's big.

Dominic laughed. Nervous. Delighted.

Arnie's hips pressed against his upturned butt. He was in. All the way.

Dominic exhaled. It took some getting used to, the utter fullness of having Arnie inside him.

Arnie put his hands on Dominic's thighs, holding him still. "Okay?"

He nodded. "I'm good."

Arnie made love to him long and slow. He seemed to appreciate Dominic's inexperience and watched him closely, gauging each move on Dominic's reaction. Gradually Dominic's body adjusted to the massive intrusion. He relaxed and allowed his thighs to spread wider. He savored the exquisite friction as Arnie thrust into him and withdrew. Dominic ran his tongue along his mouth, tasting sweat on his top lip. His skin was slick and droplets ran across his brow. His mind seemed hazy.

Arnie's cock hit a spot inside him. Each inward movement nudged his prostate, firing bolts of pleasure all through him.

Oh God. Why had he resisted this for so long? Though he loved shoving his cock into a nice arse, the satisfaction of being on the receiving end was infinitely greater.

But it had never been like this before. He was sure of it. His experiences were not extensive, but no other man had stimulated him to this degree.

Because they were the wrong men.

It was Arnie doing this to him. No one else. No one could induce such a reaction.

And it got better. Whatever was happening to his prostate, the sensations only increased, driving him crazy.

He barely knew where he was when Arnie wrapped his fist around his cock. A gentle squeeze. A slight jerk. That was all it took. Dominic went off in his hand and it seemed without end. He blew a huge white geyser, squirting over his own face. It was across his brow, in his hair. Subsequent spurts splattered hot and wet over his chest and belly. He hadn't seen so much cum since he was seventeen.

Paroxysms of pleasure gripped his entire body and wouldn't let go.

Arnie had given him the kind of orgasm he hadn't believed existed until now.

Chapter Twelve

Dominic dozed in the drowsy mid-afternoon heat, one arm draped across his belly, the other flung above his head. Arnie slipped naked from the sheets and went into the en suite bathroom, closing the door behind him. Catching his reflection in the mirror, he saw the smile writ large on his face. Everything about the image looking back at him said *just fucked*. His hair was a crazy mess and his eyes sparkled. His cheeks had the warm glow of sex and satisfaction.

The last two hours had been intense, the appetite they had for each other insatiable.

Arnie had never felt so in-tune with another man. They matched each other in every way, in hunger and desire and stamina. In his experience, no one had ever come as hard as Dominic did on the dining table. He'd been dripping with sperm afterward. It had even hung from his chin. But when Arnie had withdrawn and seen the heavy tip of the condom, he'd realized just how much seed he'd unloaded himself. He never came that much. Maybe when he young, but not these days. Not until today.

His balls must have been working overtime, because the second time had been just as intense, just as fruitful.

He'd brought Dominic up to the bedroom, where they'd taken their time, exploring each other. Dominic's body was like a compendium of every one of Arnie's fantasies. Everything he found attractive in a man had been fashioned into one perfect package. Stocky, muscular, hairy. He had thick thighs and a big, chunky arse. A well-proportioned chest and a tight belly. Dominic clearly looked after himself, but not to the point of obsession or self-denial.

In the past, Arnie had been forced to get into a particular kind of shape for a movie or TV role, especially those that required him to take his shirt off. Lose weight, get ripped, bulk up — he'd had to do it all and hated it. Maintaining that kind of physique was a joyless, unsustainable grind. Diets, restrictions, twice-daily workouts. He was all for keeping fit and staying healthy, but not in the name of looking a certain way. He was glad to see Dominic didn't fall into that trap either. He was muscular and sexy, but not to the exclusion of having a good life. Dominic had the hot body of a real man.

And what a man.

Arnie had enjoyed every inch of him, the taste and scent of his body. The blissful look that came over his face when he was getting fucked.

In bed, Dominic had reciprocated. Arnie had lain on his front while Dominic drove into him from behind, pounding him into the mattress. *Wow.* Had he ever been fucked so thoroughly? *No way.*

No wonder that face in the mirror looked so pleased with itself.

Arnie laughed, before taking a piss and washing his hands and face.

When he opened the door, Dominic was awake. He lay back, propped up on pillows, the sheets around his waist, one tanned leg sticking out.

"Hey." He grinned.

"Hey." Arnie smiled back. "Didn't disturb you, did I?"

"I was already awake."

"Fancy a drink? A beer?"

"Why not? That sounds good."

"Be right back."

Arnie pulled on his briefs and went downstairs. It was almost three o'clock. They had plenty of time. His parents wouldn't bring AJ home until at least six. He checked his phone for messages in case there had been a change of plan. Nothing. All was good. He retrieved two bottles from the refrigerator, popped the tops and hurried back upstairs to Dominic.

"You're not hungry, are you?" he asked, handing him the drink.

"Only for you," Dominic said with a wolfish grin.

Arnie went around the bed, slipped off his briefs and climbed naked beneath the sheets. "Didn't you have enough of me already?"

Dominic rolled onto his side to face him. "Of you? Are you mad? Never. When you shoved that dick in my arse, I thought I was about to split in two, that I wouldn't be able to walk afterward. And now I'm all set to go again."

Arnie laughed. "You may be. I think I need a rest first."

"I'll wait," Dominic said with a wink. "I'm just being greedy. My head is a lot more willing than my butt right now."

They both laughed loudly.

Dominic was so easygoing. So relaxed. Arnie felt no tension when he was around him. No pressure to play a part or be anything other than himself. And laughing. When had he ever been to bed with a man who made him laugh? Never.

"Did you think we'd end up here?" Arnie asked. "In bed."

"I hoped so. God, you've no idea how much I've thought about this. But I didn't want to pressure you. You've got a lot going on. So many priorities, I figured sex would be low down your list."

"It is, and it isn't. I fancied you the second I saw you, but it's true, I wasn't looking to get into anything. I resisted that desire all last week. Kept telling myself it didn't matter. I came here this summer for AJ, not to get a shag."

"You can be a good father and still get shagged."

"I know. I just don't want to fuck things up for him. It's been difficult, you know. Trying to give his life stability. The hours I work don't always fit in with childcare. I often have to leave him with childminders or arrange for him to stay with friends when I have a late shoot, or if I'm working evenings in the theatre."

"You shouldn't worry too much about that. You do a great job raising him. He's one of the politest, most intelligent kids I've met."

Arnie looked at him, searching for signs he was talking bullshit. "You mean that?"

Dominic looked straight into his eyes. "Of course I do. Just because I don't have a family of my own doesn't mean I'm totally ignorant of them. We get kids around the station all the time. School trips, families on days out. AJ stands out from the crowd."

"I hope so. I don't want to put pressure on him. I just want him to be the best he can be."

"He is, trust me. Just look at Noel."

"Noel?"

"Red-haired lad. About nineteen. He volunteers at the station. He was there when you dropped by last week."

"Oh, yes. I know who you mean." The gormless youth he'd seen several times around the marina.

"He volunteers at the station because he has to. Not from any sense of community or wanting to help. He lives with his grandparents and his grandmother makes him join in. He left school with no qualifications or experience. He hasn't got the social skills necessary to land even the most basic job. His gran asked me to look out for him, to try to draw him out and teach him some life skills. It's useless. I haven't given up trying, but I might as well tell it to the wall. The kid has no interest in improving himself. I feel he resents every minute he spends at the station. He'd rather be playing games. His grandmother can't even get the lazy bastard to sign on. If he did, at least he could offer them some money instead of always taking. So, the point I'm trying to make is that you have nothing to worry about with AJ. He's around ten years younger than Noel, but intellectually and emotionally, AJ is way ahead of him."

"What's Noel's problem? Does he have learning difficulties?"

"No. That's the annoying part. He's more than capable — he's bone-idle, simple as that. And as long as his grandparents keep handing out cash, he's got no incentive to change. I've told the old lady that, but she keeps on spoiling him. You'll never have that problem with AJ. The boy is keen to learn. He'll go far."

Arnie smiled. "It's good to hear you say that. I do the best for him, but I doubt myself all the time. And with the way his mother carries on, I feel like I'm always swimming uphill."

"Well, I wouldn't know myself, but isn't that what it's like for all parents."

Arnie nodded. "I guess it is."

He rolled onto his back and gazed at the ceiling. It was a relief, being able to talk with Dominic. He wondered why that should be. They barely knew each other, and here he was, confiding in him, revealing his insecurities. The kind of anxieties he didn't even share with his own family. It seemed to be his responsibility as a father, to hide his fears and carry on regardless.

"How do you feel about this?" he asked.

"About what? About you? Wonderful." Dominic snuggled closer across the bed.

"Getting mixed up with a single dad. I don't come without complications."

"Are you kidding? A hot daddy. That's every gay guy's fantasy right there. Pinch me, I must be dreaming."

They both chuckled.

"You mean it?" Arnie said at last.

"Mean it? I already told you. AJ's a wonderful kid. I don't have any problems with you being a dad. In case you hadn't noticed, neither of us are spring chickens. Any guy our age is going to come with some kind of history and backstory. Part of the fun will be discovering it together."

"We'll have to take things slowly. I don't want to surprise him with anything right away. His world is shaky enough without his dad dropping a boyfriend into the mix."

Dominic leaned in and kissed him on the side of his face. "You're in charge, Daddy. You set the pace. I'll wait and do things just as you want them."

Arnie rolled onto his side to face him. "Wow. Where did you come from? You appear to be the perfect man. What's the catch?"

Dominic grinned, so boyish and innocent, so different from the action hero he presented outside the bedroom. "No catch. No bullshit. I want to keep seeing you, that's all. I don't care what the terms are, that's up to you, but anything you want, I'll do it."

Dominic stayed with him until five o'clock. They remained in bed the whole time and made love again. It was less hurried and more tender than the times before. They flipped positions throughout, taking it in turns to enter each other, until it drained them.

Showered and dressed, they said goodbye in the courtyard. Arnie leaned into the open window of the car to kiss him one last time.

"I'll wait for you to call me," Dominic said. "But please, don't leave it too long."

"I won't," Arnie said, his lips lingering. He couldn't. Now that they'd gone this far, he had to have Dominic again. "I'll sound AJ out later, without giving anything away."

"If anything else happens, if that loser shows up or you're worried, call me straight away. I'll come right over. And my earlier offer still stands. If you want me on guard duty while the two of you sleep, you only have to ask."

"Thanks. I appreciate it, but I don't think it's necessary."

Dominic kissed him one last time before putting the car in gear and reversing out of the courtyard.

Chapter Thirteen

Arnie woke early the next morning and was in the kitchen preparing breakfast for AJ who was still in bed, when his mother sent a text.

Be careful when you turn on the TV. Tara is all over the news. Don't let AJ see.

For fuck's sake. What now?

In less than thirty seconds, he'd typed his ex-wife's name into a search engine and found the answer. Tara and Richie were still in Ibiza. At some point during the night, they had fallen legless out of a nightclub. Not much different from any other night, except Tara had gone flat on her arse. With her skirt around her waist and no underwear, she'd given the paparazzi exactly what they wanted. Most of the major news sites had pixilated or blurred out her crotch, but the photos left no doubt in the viewer's mind about what they were looking at. The headlines that went with the images were beyond salacious.

Tara was a laughing stock. Again.

Keeping her exploits from AJ was as tricky as fighting fire. Each day it became a bit harder. And if she continued the way she was going, there'd be no way of protecting him from this shit when he went back to school in the autumn.

Damn it! Couldn't they stop and think about someone other than themselves? Just once. The fact that AJ had witnessed an attempted murder did nothing to burst their bubble. Tara hadn't picked up the phone once in the last week to enquire after him. Not that AJ seemed bothered about her either. He hadn't mentioned his mother once.

Yesterday had gone so well too. After the wonderful afternoon with Dominic, AJ had come home around six and they'd enjoyed a laid-back evening in front of the TV with pizza and soda.

'You're in a good mood.' AJ had said as he sent him up to bed at eight thirty.

It was true. He was elated. He hadn't realized just how starved of sex — of a man — he had been. There was more to it than that. Dominic wasn't any man, and the sex was more satisfying than any casual hook-up. It had been amazing. Physically and emotionally fulfilling.

The afterglow had lasted all night, and he still felt the effect of it this morning. Arnie was certain he had woken up with a smile on his face.

It had been *that* good.

Now Tara and Richie's antics in Ibiza had taken the shine off it.

If he could keep the pictures from AJ, they might not ruin the day.

As the kettle boiled, Arnie went into the study. This had become a morning ritual. He turned on the CCTV monitor and watched the footage from when he went to bed, around eleven p.m. He brought up all the cameras and reviewed the material at a speeded-up frame rate, whizzing through the hours until dawn. He paid most attention to the front of the house, where the stalker had first appeared.

Nothing. Not so much as a cat or fox passing by.

Thank God for that. He wasn't sure how he'd react if he saw the stalker on screen.

Yes, he knew. He would pack their cases and leave town immediately.

There were lots of reasons to stay in Nyemouth for the summer, but the risk wasn't worth it.

He would take one day at a time and be prepared for anything.

There were footsteps above as AJ trod heavily to the bathroom. Arnie shut off the monitor and left the study, closing the door behind him. He was waiting in the kitchen when AJ came down, his hair all over the place.

"Can I watch *Batman*?" he asked, holding up a DVD.

"Sure you can," Arnie said, grateful he didn't have to think of a distraction to keep AJ away from the news. "Let me set it up for you."

He turned on the TV and DVD player and left AJ happily watching the superhero while he got on with breakfast. He made a large plate of bacon sandwiches for them to share and sat on the sofa next to AJ with fresh orange juice. The boy was so caught up in the action on screen that he barely spoke.

"Eat up before it gets cold," Arnie said, trying to break the spell of the cartoon.

He realized, in the sobering light of the morning, that he had to consider his priorities — AJ and keeping him safe. As hung-up on Dominic as he'd become, he couldn't let him get in the way. Yesterday had made him appreciate, more than ever, that he missed the dynamic of an adult relationship and the intimacy of being with another man. He'd denied himself for too long. It was bound to resurface at some point. Such a basic human need couldn't be ignored forever. But the timing was all wrong. He couldn't get distracted by a love affair. Not now. Not when Tara was behaving like the world's biggest idiot and a masked man had been hanging around the house.

Fuck it. What where they even doing here? He knew what he should do. Pack up and take AJ abroad for the summer. Out of the country, where no one could find them. That had to be the answer. They could always return to Nyemouth in the autumn if the police caught the man responsible. *And if not?* They would stay away for good. His parents would have to come to London when they wanted to see their grandson. They would manage.

And Dominic?

Forget him.

Arnie knew he couldn't, but for the sake of his son, he might have to.

"How do you fancy going to Disneyland?" he asked.

AJ didn't take his eyes off the screen. "In America?"

"Sure."

"No."

"Why not? You'd love it."

"I don't want to go on an aeroplane."

"Oh." This was news. "You've flown before, don't you remember? When you were little."

"I remember," he said, still engrossed in *Batman*. "I didn't like it."

"What about Disneyland Paris? That's a lot closer. We could even drive that far. Or take a train. We wouldn't have to fly." The idea of driving all that way seemed like a massive drag, but if that was what it took to get AJ away, it would be a small price.

"When?"

"I don't know. I can look at tickets today and we could leave as early as tomorrow. How about that?"

Now AJ tore his eyes away from the screen. "I thought you meant, like half-term in October. Not now."

"What's wrong with now? Don't you like the idea."

He shook his head. "We're supposed to be here for the summer. I've got plans."

"What plans?"

"I'm having a sleepover with Conner and Indina at their house tomorrow night. And then they're staying here for the weekend and bringing Benji over."

He couldn't help laughing. "When was all this decided?"

"Yesterday." He returned his attention to *Batman*.

"I guess that means we're staying here."

AJ patted his father's knee. "We can still go to Disneyland in October. If that's what you really want."

* * * *

They spent the day in the Newcastle, the closest major city. He took AJ to a dinosaur exhibition at the Natural History Museum and followed it up with a movie matinee. The film about a giant shark seemed a little on the scary side to Arnie, but AJ loved every minute and wouldn't shut up about it when he took him to a burger bar for food afterward.

It was a great day and went some way to easing the earlier apprehensions he'd had about staying put. AJ seemed unaffected by everything that was going on around him. Maybe Arnie should just accept that and let him get on with enjoying the summer. He could always insist on taking him back to London if the situation changed.

For today at least, everything seemed good.

"Dad, can I watch *King Kong* before I go to bed?" AJ asked on the drive back to Nyemouth. He was sitting in the rear seat playing with the plastic T-Rex he'd begged Arnie to buy him at the museum.

"No, it's too long. You can watch it tomorrow if that's what you want. Why don't you take it with you to the sleepover, then you can all watch it?"

The idea seemed to please him. "Excellent."

Arnie watched him in the mirror, absorbed with his dinosaur. Another day had gone by and he'd managed to protect him from the salacious press coverage his mother's behavior had attracted. Arnie happily took the small win.

"Dad?" AJ asked, as they drove north up the A1. "Why don't you have a boyfriend?"

The question startled him. Arnie tried not to show it. "I just don't, son. I'm too busy for a boyfriend."

The answer seemed to sit for a moment before AJ came back, "Don't you think you should have one by now? At your age?"

"At my age? How ancient do you think I am?"

"Not that old, but most grown-ups have someone, don't they?"

"Not everybody. Some people are on their own. And that's fine too. Where did this question come from?"

"Nowhere. We were just talking, that's all."

"Who are *we*?" Arnie asked.

"Connor and Indina. They think you should get a boyfriend, and so do I."

Arnie couldn't help but laugh. "You have it all figured out. Do you have anyone special in mind, or am I allowed to choose for myself?"

"Indina says Gabriel is nice. From The Lobster Pot."

Jesus, these guys had given this some proper thought. "Gabriel is nice," he said, cautious, wondering where to take this next. "But he's my friend. We went to school together. I couldn't be his boyfriend."

"Why not?"

Oh God. "There's just...no romance between us, that's all."

"And does there have to be romance for you to be boyfriends?" AJ asked, looking at him in the rearview mirror.

"There does, yes. Lots of romance. And that's just for a start. Why don't you forget it, eh? If I do find a boyfriend, I promise to let you know. How does that sound?"

AJ shrugged. "Whatever."

They got home after seven. Arnie ran AJ a bath, and while he was soaking and playing shark versus dinosaur with his toys, Arnie checked the CCTV cameras. There was no sign of anything out of the ordinary.

He felt nervous about the house. It had seemed so secure when he had chosen it, and obviously it was — he had to remind himself of that — but seeing that guy creeping around the other night had unsettled him. Arnie hated it, paying so much attention their security and protection all the time. Unlike other celebrities, he'd never been the type to obsess about those things.

Even when he was making big-budget movies and was the flavor of the moment, he'd always been relaxed about it, living in regular houses and apartments. Of course, he'd been on his own then.

Having AJ changed his outlook on everything.

He would check the cameras several more times before turning in that night — he knew that for a fact.

Maybe it would be different if he weren't on his own.

If there were two men in the house instead of one.

And if the other guy were an ex-special forces officer, there would be nothing to fear at all.

AJ was tired after their day out. By eight thirty he was in bed and asleep. Arnie eased the dinosaur toy from his tight grip and put it on the side table. He left the night-light on and the door ajar before going back downstairs.

And now he was all alone, pacing the floors.

What the hell was wrong? Being alone had never bothered him before. At home there would often be lines to learn in the evening, and if not, he would read a book or watch a film or TV series. There were a million things he could do to occupy himself. Right now, the temptation was to go back into the damn study and check the CCTV.

No way. He refused to go down the route of paranoia. It would never end.

But the house was so large and empty around him. Wandering through the living room and kitchen, all he saw were sparse surfaces and clear spaces. As he poured a small glass of wine, AJ's earlier question ran through his mind. *'Why don't you have a boyfriend?'*

Good question, son. And what's the real answer? Because I'm scared. Because I won't allow it. I'm stubborn. I'm stupid. Because there's no romance in my life.

Whose fault is that?

Nobody but his own. He made excuses. Created obstacles. Like AJ. Like Tara. The press. Bad publicity.

It was all crap.

Tomorrow AJ was going to his cousins' for a sleepover.

He wondered for a second whether the kids had planned it that way. Maybe when they'd had their little discussion about his personal life and lack of a significant other. Had AJ arranged his own childcare so he wouldn't have to?

No, that was ridiculous. They were children — they didn't think about such things.

But it gave him a night off. With nothing to do in the big empty house.

Before he could change his mind, Arnie picked up the phone and called Dominic.

Chapter Fourteen

It had been a quiet couple of weeks for the crew of the lifeboat. The weather had remained good throughout, with glorious sunshine most days and temperatures well above what Nyemouth and the whole of the Northumbrian coast was used to. Tourists continued to pour into the town to enjoy the beaches and parks. There was an increase in sailing boats passing in and out of the harbor, and the rocky coastline was thronged with opportunistic line-fishermen. The recent publicity over Sandy Costello and the attack she'd suffered on the cliff had drawn a few morbidly minded visitors, keen to see the spot where it had happened and perhaps witness a new assault.

Despite all of this, there were no fresh emergency call-outs for over a week and a half.

Dominic was at home when his pager went off a little after two o'clock on Friday. He'd spent a productive morning working on his novel, hitting his two-thousand-word count with ease. He'd taken

Brandy for a walk, enjoyed a lunch of smoked mackerel with bread and butter, and was about to tackle a bunch of weeds in the garden when the call was raised.

Racing along the terrace and down the steps to the marina, he was the third person to arrive at the station. The front doors were open and the boat was already being prepared for launch.

"What is it?" he asked, stepping into his life-preserving suit.

"Two kids in a dinghy," answered Ronan, climbing to the wheel of the tractor that would launch the boat as soon as a full crew was on site.

"Where?"

"Somewhere off North Point. They drifted away from the beach and the off-shore wind is carrying them out."

"Do we know how old they are?"

"Eleven and twelve," Ronan answered.

Two further crew members arrived at the station — Haig, a fifty-seven-year-old veteran, and Joanne, who was in her midtwenties and had only recently completed her mandatory sea training. They had enough to launch. Joanne had only been on one previous shout, but they couldn't waste time waiting for a more experienced volunteer to arrive. Not with two kids on the water.

Dominic climbed into the boat and took his seat at the helm. Haig and Joanne joined him a minute later, fully kitted up with their helmets on. Ronan backed the trailer down the ramp into the water. Dominic eased the boat out gently until they were clear, before motoring across the harbor at speed. As they left the shelter of the marina, he opened up the engines and headed north into open sea.

Though it had looked tranquil from the shore, there was a stiff breeze on the water and a two-meter swell caused the boat to rise and fall as he sped along the coast.

Accidents at sea could occur in the mildest of weather. Too many people underestimated the conditions. The swell would make the tiny dinghy difficult to spot, and with the strength of the wind, he could only guess at where they would be now. Without knowing the exact time they had gotten into trouble, his only option was to head for the spot where they'd last been seen and take it from there.

More information came through his earpiece en route. The kids had been playing at the northernmost end of the point.

"When were they last seen?" He had to shout over the noise of the engines and the howling wind.

"Thirteen-twenty-five," came the reply.

They had been missing for over an hour.

"The wind will have taken them east," Haig shouted from his position up front. He gestured to the horizon. "Straight out."

"Agreed," Dominic said, adjusting course.

The idea of two children being lost in a vast, open sea was sickening. Dominic couldn't let his emotions or fears get in the way. Adrenaline surged through him, but he had almost two decades' experience and knew how to control it. He focused on the task at hand — finding the kids and getting them safely home.

However hopeless that might appear.

The children's greatest chance of survival was if they remained in the dinghy. If their flimsy vessel had been blown over, or they tried to swim back to shore, the odds were massively against them.

The North Sea was cold all year round, even in the height of summer. Exposure to the water without a wetsuit could be fatal after a few minutes, and children of that age wouldn't have the strength to hold themselves up for much longer than that.

They would be fine as long as they were still in the boat and could be found in time.

The wind and the swell increased the farther out they traveled. Dominic handled the boat while his crewmates kept their eyes trained on the surface for anything that might suggest a small craft.

With every passing minute, the situation became more desperate.

"There," Haig shouted. "Five o'clock."

Dominic turned the boat in the direction Haig was pointing. "Do you see them?" he called back.

"Saw something," he answered. "Lost sight again in the swell, but there's definitely something out there."

Dominic followed the course, trusting the other man's intuition. Spotting a person or a small craft like a dinghy or a kayak in ever-shifting waves was nigh on impossible. The object could be there for no more than a second, then gone, never seen again.

On the next rising wave, Dominic caught sight of a dark shape low in the water, about a mile distant. It was swallowed by the downward swell. He adjusted course, heading straight for it.

"It's them," Joanne called a moment later, relief clear in her voice. "Both boys. They're still in the dinghy."

"Thank Christ."

As the distance closed between them, he saw them for the first time.

Two young kids wearing swimming shorts waved at the lifeboat, their faces ash-gray. The dinghy they were in was tiny, fit for nothing more than a backyard paddling pool, totally unworthy of the open sea. It sickened him that two boys had almost lost their lives in a piece of crap that cost no more than a few quid at their local supermarket.

The lecture could wait until later — getting them onto the bigger boat and warmed up was the priority.

"Have either of you been in the water?" Joanne asked as they drew alongside.

The boys shook their heads. Their eyes were wide and frightened. Haig leaned over and held their dinghy secure, while Joanne helped them across. Their teeth chattered with the cold as they huddled down in the bow. Joanne swaddled them in blankets while Haig hauled their puny dinghy over the side. Without a pause, he took a knife from the emergency box and stabbed it straight into the dinghy. Dominic looked on with satisfaction as it deflated and withered in the bottom of the boat.

While the others checked out the boys, he radioed to shore. "Both parties found safe and well. Suggest a paramedic is waiting upon return to check for hypothermia. ETA fifteen minutes."

Wrapped in the thermal blankets and hunkered in the front of the boat, the kids looked a lot better than when they had found them. A little color had come back to their faces, though their eyes were wide with fright.

He took the return journey at a steady pace, allowing Haig and Joanne to monitor their charges. It appeared no serious harm had been done, but they had to be checked for signs of shock and hypothermia, both of which were killers. The boys were called Billy and Joshua. They were brothers. In a childlike rush, they explained how they'd been at the beach with their parents. They'd been playing on the shore with their dinghy and by the time they'd realized the tide had carried them out, it was too late to get back. As hard as they'd paddled, the current and wind had taken them in the opposite direction.

A typical story. Dominic had heard it plenty of times before. Visitors to the coast, unused to the area, approached the sea with naivety and ignorance, believing it was no different from the warm Mediterranean they were used to from their holidays. They had no clue about tides, currents, local danger spots. Most callouts received by the lifeboat were for cases exactly like this.

Billy and Joshua had had one hell of a scare. Looking at them now, he doubted they would go near the water for a very long time. He'd spare them a telling-off when they reached the shore. They were frightened enough.

As he maneuvered the boat through the marina, Dominic was pleased to see the flashing blue lights of an ambulance waiting by the station. The kids would be taken off immediately. It wasn't always the case. During peak periods, they'd had to treat casualties with first aid kits for upward of three hours while waiting for a paramedic crew to arrive.

The tractor was already in position on the ramp, with the trailer waiting in the water. He backed the boat onto the frame, and once it was secure, they were towed up to the station. A small crowd gathered to watch the process. Billy and Joshua gazed warily at the curious faces turned in their direction.

"Don't worry about them," he assured the brothers, lifting the young boy out of the boat and into the care of the paramedic team.

Haig gave the medics a summary of what had happened and the boys' condition. A woman rushed forward to be with them. Her face was drawn and almost as gray as the kids' when they'd found them. She was obviously their mother.

Jacob stood in the open door of the station with Brandy on a lead beside him. Noel was there too, pulling out the hose to clean the salt water from the boat. The lad was showing some initiative. Until now, he'd always had to be told what to do. Maybe he would make the crew someday.

"Good work," Jacob said, coming forward.

Brandy nudged his thigh, open-mouthed and panting. Dominic stroked her head. "They were lucky."

"What was it?"

"A shitty dinghy."

Jacob grimaced. "About time the bloody things were outlawed."

At that moment, a man in baggy shorts and a red football shirt came over. His complexion was ruddy and the jersey was stretched tight across the huge swell of his gut. "Where's the boat?" he asked.

Dominic looked him over carefully. The impression he got was not a good one. The man was balding and unkempt, his hard-faced features suggested a short temper. "Excuse me?"

"You brought them back, didn't you? What happened to their boat?"

"Who are you?" Dominic kept a neutral tone.

"I'm their dad," the man said, squaring his shoulders.

"Oh. Well, congratulations. You must be relieved to have your boys back safely. That was a dangerous situation they got themselves into. It might easily have turned to disaster. As it was, it's given them a big fright. I don't think they'll be in any hurry to go back on the water, but before they do, I'd suggest you drop by here first. Bring them along and one of our volunteers will be happy to take them through the basics of water safety."

The man's mouth opened and closed a couple of times before any words came out. "But what about their boat? It's brand new. I only bought it for them yesterday."

"Oh, right." Dominic stepped up onto the trailer and reached into the lifeboat. He flung the tattered piece of rubber at the man's feet. "It got punctured on the way in. I'd save my money if I was you, mate. Not worth buying another one. You can see what a cheap piece of shit it is. Not fit for purpose."

The man let out a pitiful sigh, staring at the ruined dinghy.

Arsehole.

Dominic went into the station to write his report on the rescue before he said anything he might regret.

* * * *

An hour later, the lifeboat had been cleaned and replenished with emergency blankets, Dominic had completed the paperwork and the crew had enjoyed a cup of tea together in the kitchen. It was an informal kind of debrief, necessary to celebrate the success of the call and get their adrenaline levels back to normal before continuing with their day. As the head of the boat that afternoon, he was keen to commend Joanne for her good work. It was important to encourage the new members, and she deserved the praise.

"You did brilliantly well," he said.

Afterward Jacob told Dominic to go home. "I'll lock up the station. There are a couple of things I want to take Noel through before I go. No need for you to stay."

He accepted the offer gratefully. Arnie had called yesterday to say AJ was going on a sleepover with his cousins, meaning he was free for the entire night. Dominic could barely contain his elation. Arnie had said he needed to take things slowly, so he'd decided to step back and let Arnie come to him when he was ready. He'd never expected see him so soon.

'What do you want to do?' he'd asked. *'We could go out for a meal. Or do you want me to come over?'*

'I want to get out of this house for a while,' Arnie had said. *'But I'm not ready to go anywhere public. Not when Tara is still grabbing headlines. Could I come to you?'*

They'd made plans for Arnie to get to Dominic's house around six thirty, after he'd dropped off AJ. The rescue had taken a big chunk out of the afternoon, but Dominic still had time to tidy around the house, take a shower and get cleaned up before Arnie arrived. It was probably just as well he'd been so busy. If not, the anticipation might have driven him crazy.

Spending time with Arnie would make this the most exciting Friday night he'd had in years.

With Brandy at his side, he walked out of the station. It looked like the beginning of a decent enough evening. The stiff breeze they'd experienced at sea remained there. The temperature in the town was pleasant and the sky was clear. If it stayed that way, he and Arnie could sit in the garden for a while and enjoy a nice alfresco drink.

Drinks – of course. Arnie had a thing for white wine, while Dominic couldn't remember ever having a bottle in the house. Only whiskey and beer.

"Better pay a visit to the off license," he said to the dog.

Brandy wagged her tail and gazed at him, her tongue lolling from her mouth.

There was a wine shop on the other side of the marina, a few doors along from The Lobster Pot. Pricey, he imagined, but they could advise him on what to buy.

As he crossed in front of the restaurant, Gabriel came out of the door. It was the first he'd seen of him since their confrontation at the fair last weekend.

"Hi there," Dominic said, with no intention of stopping. He'd said what he needed to the other day — there was no point raking over it again.

"Well done," Gabriel said, stepping forward. "I heard about the kids this afternoon. Good call."

Dominic drew a deep breath and stopped, turning to look at him. "Thanks. It was luck more than anything. We got the kids home, that's all that matters."

Gabriel came closer. He was dressed in black, narrow-legged trousers and an open-necked shirt. His regular outfit for work. "How are things with Arnie?"

Oh boy, here it comes again.

Dominic spoke as evenly as he had with the father of the rescued boys. "We went over this before, Gabriel. There's nothing else to say on the subject."

"But you are fucking him, right?"

"It has nothing to do with you. I told you — you and I, we were never an item. End of story."

Gabriel crossed his arms over his chest. His handsome face was marred by the expression of a petulant child. "I don't think the press would see it that way. Do you?"

"What's that supposed to mean?"

"Exactly what it sounds like." Gabriel took another step forward. His voice was low and vicious. "I've been thinking. It's a big story. Huge. Look at Tara, she's in the papers every day of the week. They can't get enough of the scandal. But it's all one-sided at the minute. Every detail of her love life put out for everyone to enjoy. I'll bet some of those papers would enjoy evening things up a little. Running a piece or two about Arnie Walker. Seeing what Tara's ex is up to while she's flashing herself around Ibiza."

Dominic stared at him. There was pure spite in Gabriel's eyes.

"Why would you do that?" he asked calmly.

"I'm sure the story is worth a few grand to the morning rags. Why shouldn't I benefit from it?"

"You don't need the money."

"That's no reason to turn it down. Besides, who doesn't need money?"

"C'mon, what good will it do you? Once word gets around. You rely on the people here to get you through the winter. You'll be crucified if you sell Arnie out."

"That's only because everyone thinks he's a nice guy. Mr. Perfect. With his looks and money and photogenic kid. If I tell the story right, I could do a fair amount of damage to that clean-cut reputation of his. Yours too. I'm the wronged man here, remember. You cheated on me with Mr. Wonderful. He waltzed into town and stole you from me."

"That's not what happened."

"It makes a good story."

"I'll ask again. Why? What do you hope to gain from it?"

"Satisfaction. Justice. Revenge. I can go on."

Dominic shook his head. "Wow. I thought I knew you. I thought you were a decent man. This goes to show how wrong I was. Arnie too. He thinks you're his friend."

"How do you know that?" Gabriel said, his eyes flashing, his voice getting harder with anger. "Have you been talking about me, eh? The two of you snuggled up, having a good laugh at my expense. Was it pillow talk? Did you talk about me in bed, eh? Tell him all about our affair after you fucked him?"

"Why are you behaving like this? I told Arnie about you so there would be no secrets between us. I wanted to be upfront with him. Just like I was with you. For the hundredth time, you and I were fuck buddies. That was the deal, and I never promised you anything more."

Gabriel unfolded his arms. His fists were clenched in fury. "How fucking dare you? How dare you tell me Arnie is my friend, when he jumped on you, that dick of yours, knowing all about me? That's not what friends do."

"And this is? Threatening to sell bullshit stories to the press out of spite. Arnie knew there was nothing between you and me. I told him the truth. That we had an agreement and nothing more. Jesus," he said, exasperated. "I won't make the same damn mistake. So much for no-strings fun. This is the exact opposite of that."

"You had your fun, all right. Now it's my turn. I'll sell the fucking story and I'll take the money. I deserve it after all I've been through."

"You'll regret it," Dominic said coldly.

Brandy, agitated by the anger in their voices, let out a bark.

"Are you threatening me?" Gabriel said with defiance.

"I'm just stating a fact. You do such a cruel, underhand thing and you'll hurt a lot of people, including yourself."

"I've been hurt enough," Gabriel snarled. "It's your new fuck buddy who'll be crying this time."

Dominic had heard enough. Tugging on Brandy's lead, he turned his back on Gabriel and walked away.

"I'll do it," Gabriel shouted after him. "Don't think I won't."

Keeping control of his temper, Dominic didn't stop. They were done.

Chapter Fifteen

When Arnie dropped AJ off at his sister's, the boy rushed toward the house with his overnight bag, filled with games, toys and DVDs.

"Not so fast," Arnie called, hurrying after him.

"What?" AJ said, almost at the front door.

"Give your dad a hug before you go." Arnie crouched to match his height.

AJ put down the bag and opened his arms. Arnie hugged him tight, breathing in the familiar smell of him.

"Behave for Aunt Sophie," he warned.

"I will."

"And don't stay up too late."

"Dad, it's a sleepover. We have to stay up late."

The front door opened and AJ rushed inside, pushing straight past Sophie.

She laughed. "He's keen."

"Sorry." Arnie leaned in to kiss her on the cheek. "I did my best to tire him out this afternoon, but I don't think it worked. He's as high as a kite."

"He'll be in good company. Conner and Indina are just as excited."

"Are you sure you don't mind doing this? I can always call back for him later."

Sophie put a hand on his chest, pushing him away. "Go. Have a great night and we'll see you in the morning. Not too early either. Make sure you get a good lie-in. You deserve it."

"Thanks, sis," he said, backing down the path. "Call me if you change your mind."

"Stop worrying. Forget about everything and have a fantastic night." She added, with a smirk, "I know I would. You lucky sod."

"What's that supposed to mean?"

"You know what it means," she said cheekily. "Now have fun with your sexy hero and I'll see you tomorrow. No earlier than noon."

Sophie closed the door before he could reply further.

Something had obviously been said about him and Dominic. First AJ's comments about getting a boyfriend and now this. He thought they'd been discreet. He should have known better, especially when he'd lived here before. Nyemouth was a small town and nothing stayed secret for long in a place like this. No doubt someone had seen Dominic at his house, either arriving or leaving.

He got back into the car and locked the doors. Security was still high on the agenda. The drive to Dominic's took less than five minutes. *Now people will really have something to gossip about*, he thought, as he parked his car outside Dominic's. He didn't care. He needed some time away from Cliff House, just for a few hours.

The front door opened and Dominic appeared as Arnie stepped onto the garden path. He was stunning, dressed in a white linen shirt and dark chinos, his feet bare. Just as before, the sight of him caused something in Arnie to flip. In an instant, he felt young, giddy and carefree. As if the clock had been turned back twenty years, he was a teenager again with his whole life ahead of him.

Arnie waited until they were inside before wrapping his arms around him. They held each other, chins resting on their shoulders.

"I heard there was a rescue this afternoon," Arnie said. "Did everything work out okay?"

"Just fine," Dominic said, sliding his hands down Arnie's back until they rested softly on his waist. "A couple of kids got into trouble, but they're home now and safe in their own beds tonight."

"I took AJ up to the Natural History Museum in Newcastle today. He hasn't stopped talking about it all week and wanted to see the dinosaurs again. The lifeboat was back in the station when we returned, but my dad told us you'd been out. I'd glad it went well."

A dog came along the hall, its claws clicking on the wooden floors, head raised to inspect the newcomer.

"This is Brandy," Dominic said, breaking their hold.

Arnie put a hand out to stroke her head. The dog nudged it happily. "Hello, Brandy."

"Looks like you passed the test," Dominic said. "Come on through. Let's get something to drink. Oh, and mind your head."

Though the interior of the house had been modernized, several of the doorways were low and Arnie had to stoop to pass through them. It was a typical feature in houses of this age. "You did all the work in here yourself?" Arnie asked, noting how sympathetic the modernization had been to the original building. "It's beautiful."

"All but the wiring and some plumbing jobs."

The kitchen was small, but one wall had been taken out to put in French windows leading onto a patio, bringing in a lot of light and the illusion of space. Satisfied that her master's visitor posed no threat, Brandy padded onto the patio and flopped, head resting on her paws, to catch the last of the day's sunshine.

Dominic opened the refrigerator. "I got wine," he said, brandishing a bottle. "No idea what it is, but the guy in the shop recommended it." He showed Arnie the label. It was a French chardonnay.

"Looks perfect."

Dominic picked a wineglass off the draining board. "I had to borrow this from Jacob next door. I don't own any wineglasses either."

"You shouldn't have gone to all this trouble."

"I'm a beer and whiskey man. That's all I usually have in." He filled the glass for Arnie and opened a bottle of beer for himself. "Want to sit outside for a while? The view out back isn't so good, but it is private. If we go out front, anyone walking by will see you."

"The back will be fine." The garden was small, just big enough for the patio and a border, before the rocky edges of South Cliff stretched above them. "Wow," Arnie said, "this *is* private."

A high fence to the right blocked the view of Jacob Chisholm's garden. Jacob would have to crane his neck from one of the upper windows to see what was happening below. They sat on an L-shaped patio sofa and put their drinks on a low table.

"We'll lose the sun in half an hour," Dominic explained. "But I can light the fire pit over there if it gets cold, or we can go inside."

Arnie raised his glass. "Cheers."

"Cheers." Dominic tapped the neck of his bottle against the glass and drank.

The wine was good. Arnie murmured his appreciation.

"It's perfect up here," he said. "I mean the house, this garden, how private it is. No wonder you fell in love with the place."

"I do love it. I like the town, but it's good to be slightly removed from it. Perched up here with just a handful of neighbours suits me."

Arnie leaned back into the sofa. "It's a small town all right, with all the good and bad things that come with it. I haven't told a soul I was coming here tonight, but when I dropped AJ at my sister's, she seemed to know all about it. I sometimes think the walls have eyes and ears in this town."

Dominic turned to look at him, his mouth set in a serious line. "Mmm," he said. "I wasn't sure how to approach this. But seeing how you brought it up, now seems as good a time as any. It's Gabriel."

"What about him? I haven't seen him since Sunday. I've been meaning to call on him, but with everything else going on and that guy hanging around the house, it slipped my mind."

Dominic gestured to the wineglass. "You might want to take a drink for this. Gabriel is pissed. Very pissed. If people are gossiping, I'd say it's likely the stories came from him. I don't know how well you know him, but it has to be a damn sight better than me.

He threatened to go to the press and tell them about us. About you and me."

Arnie reached for the wine. "You're right. I do need this. Did he say why?"

"Well, like I said, he's pissed off. He's accused me of dropping him in favor of you. Which is bullshit, because there was nothing between me and him to drop. I don't know if it's his pride or his ego. Whether he's even serious about going through with it. Considering you've known him all these years, it seems so unlikely. Then again, I never would have expected him to come out with a threat like that. I thought I should warn you first, in case you open the papers one morning and see yourself all over them."

"Oh bugger," he sighed. "It's one thing after another lately."

"Sorry. It's the last thing you needed to hear. You've got enough on your plate. I'll talk to him again tomorrow. He should have calmed down. Maybe he'll see sense."

"No," Arnie said. "If he's pissed at you, it might make things worse. Let me do it. I might be able to talk sense into him. Thirty years of history must count for something, right?"

"I hope so." Dominic swallowed his beer. "If I'd known you were about to come into my life, I'd never have gotten involved with him. From the way he's acting, I wish I hadn't anyway. I hate all this drama. It's a pointless waste of energy."

As they spoke, Arnie's eyes drifted to the open neck of Dominic's shirt. The top three buttons were undone, revealing plenty of the fur-covered muscle beneath. *God, he's sexy.* Arnie couldn't help himself. But he had to take it slow, not rush things.

It doesn't have to be complicated, remember. No one said this had to be anything more than it was right now. Two men getting to know one another, having fun along the way. Maybe it would lead to something — most likely it wouldn't. What harm could there be in finding out?

Dominic asked questions about AJ and seemed to have a genuine interest in the answers. How was he doing at school? What kind of subjects was he interested in? Did he take after his mother or his father?

"It's obvious he gets his looks from you," Dominic remarked.

"Thankfully, a lot more than looks. I don't think I could handle a miniature version of Tara too well. AJ's a good kid. If he stays on the straight and narrow like his dad, I'll be very happy."

"I don't know. His dad doesn't seem all that straight to me," Dominic said, his brown eyes twinkling.

Arnie laughed. "That's true. AJ can turn out any way he likes, really — I just want him to be happy and stay healthy. His mother is an addict. If he inherits anything from her, I don't want it to be that aspect of her personality."

"I'll drink to that," Dominic said, raising his glass.

As predicted, the sun moved away from the patio, and with it, so did the evening warmth. It reminded Arnie that they were sitting on a hillside on the North East coast of England, not the south of France. Dominic lit the fire pit and, while waiting for the flames to take hold, he replenished their drinks.

"How about some music?" he asked.

"Perfect."

He went inside, and after a minute a song began to play through the open doors. Arnie recognized the singer's voice but not the song. Dominic returned with a couple of takeaway menus. "I can't cook, so let's order something to be delivered."

"What's the music?" Arnie asked, liking the sound.

"Jack Savoretti," he answered. "I'm old school. All my music is on CD or vinyl. I don't do streaming. I like to own something physical."

"Sounds good to me," Arnie said.

After browsing the menus, they settled on pizza and garlic bread. Dominic phoned the order in.

"They say it will take at least an hour," he said, getting off the phone. "It's a busy night. You're not hungry, are you? If you are, I can always make a sandwich."

Arnie looked at him intently. "I'm not hungry for anything except you."

Dominic grinned. "Is that a corny line from one of your movies?"

Arnie shook his head, getting to his feet. "No, it's especially for you."

"Then I hope they take their time with the pizza delivery."

They came together in the middle of the patio, throwing their arms around each other, their mouths joining. Arnie slid his hands straight beneath Dominic's linen shirt, getting a feel for his hot, naked skin, desperate to reconnect with him. Wanting to get reacquainted with the shape of Dominic's body, the muscle of his shoulders, the thickness of his waist, the intoxicating smell of him, the insistent push of his erection.

Dominic propelled him toward the patio sofa.

"Hang on," Arnie said, still holding on to him. "I think we should go inside. It's bad enough my ex-wife is in all the papers cavorting with her man. I don't want to join her on the front pages."

"No one can see us out here. It's private."

"I'd rather not take that risk."

Dominic planted his hand on Arnie's arse and led him inside. It was over-precautious, Arnie knew it was, but why take the risk? Sex with Dominic would be just as exciting indoors as out. Dominic guided him down the hall, into a living room. Arnie noted another low ceiling, the fireplace and the furniture, before Dominic dropped to his haunches and got to work on his belt and zipper.

Arnie stood still, allowing Dominic to do what he wanted. It was an insane turn-on, seeing a big, beefy guy on his knees, his eyes glazed with passion and hunger, tearing at his trousers with impatience. Dominic yanked Arnie's underwear and trousers to his knees, freeing his hard and heavy cock. Arnie's shirt spoiled the view, so he pulled it over his head and tossed it onto the sofa. Now he could see everything.

Dominic took his time. He had both of his hands on Arnie's thighs. He tilted his head as he gazed at his cock, seeming to admire it from different angles. Arnie pulled up his muscles, causing his cock to jerk just inches from Dominic's face. Dominic licked his lips.

"Are you trying to tease me?" he asked.

"Just showing off," Arnie replied, twitching his manhood again.

The anticipation was killing him. His foreskin retracted, revealing the glistening, dark pink head beneath. Dominic moved his hand upward, stroking his inner thighs. His fingertips grazed the underside of Arnie's balls. Arnie gasped. His scrotum tightened and gooseflesh prickled all over.

Dominic took his balls in a firm grip and moved his face closer to Arnie's cock. Hot breath seared over the head as he came closer, closer. Arnie held his breath in anticipation. Dominic looked up at him, locking him in a gaze, wordlessly expressing their mutual need and desire. Then his lips brushed against the head.

"Ugh." Arnie shuddered, his entire body reacting to the touch.

Dominic held Arnie in his mouth. He took his time, and Arnie savored the moment. Arnie widened his stance, giving it up, putting complete trust in the man beneath him. Dominic moved his hands to Arnie's arse and drew him in. Arnie groaned and ran his fingers through Dominic's thick brown hair. It was obvious what Dominic wanted and he was happy to oblige. As an actor, he'd lost count of the offers he'd had from strangers who wanted to do exactly this. Arnie rarely took them up for the simple reason that it was never like this. Dominic wasn't looking for a story to tell his friends, about blowing the film star. They were equals here, connected.

Arnie found it difficult to stop the rise. His breathing became rapid, uneven.

Dominic released him for a moment. "Don't hold back. I want to taste you. We've got all night to take things further." He took Arnie in his mouth again and resumed sucking.

"Oh God," Arnie said, losing control. "Do it. Take it out of me."

Dominic's head moved faster, smooth and wet, with not a trace of snagging.

Arnie gave a massive roar as he came. His head spun and he felt sure he was about to topple over. He was reduced to a spurting wreck and just about managed to stay upright. Dominic kept him in his mouth all the way, sucking until there was nothing left and Arnie's cock began to soften.

At last, Dominic sank onto his haunches, a self-satisfied grin written large across his face. "I think you've been saving that all week. Just for me?"

Arnie ruffled his hair. "Are you always so knowledgeable? I thought I kept a good secret."

Dominic licked his lips. "Nobody could ever keep a load like that secret."

Arnie murmured agreement. "Now get your own pants off. Let's see what you've been saving for me."

* * * *

Gabriel closed the restaurant at twelve. The bar would remain open until one, but he didn't need to stay for that. His staff could take care of things. It had been a busy night of service, right up until the cut-off for orders at ten thirty. It was just as well. He'd needed to keep busy. To keep his mind occupied. To stop him thinking about the mess he'd made with Dominic that afternoon.

When he remembered the things he'd said, the spiteful threats he'd made, he cringed.

What an arse.

It was little wonder Dominic had looked so pissed. Almost as pissed as Gabriel was with himself right now. *Jesus, you idiot.*

He checked on the bar staff, who assured him everything was fine, and said goodnight.

Escaping into the cool night air, he took a deep breath through his mouth. He heard laugher and the thumping bass of music from the direction of the town center, but the marina was all closed, other than his bar. As much as he'd appreciated the hustle of a crowded Friday, it was a relief to embrace the stillness and relative quiet of the night. Even the inky black water in the harbor was still. He turned and sauntered toward the car park.

As he thought about Dominic again, he let out a long groan.

How the hell could he make things right between them?

And Arnie? If Dominic told him a fraction of the things he'd said, it would ruin their friendship.

He hadn't meant any of it. He'd been angry. An irrational mess, lashing out at an easy target. What for? *Because you're bloody jealous, that's why.*

Gabriel got into his car. The sexy voice of Jack Savoretti came over the sound system as he turned on the engine, and made him think of Dominic again. He'd introduced him to Jack's music. For a moment he was tempted to turn the car up the hill and head over to Dominic's. The song only made him want him more. But no. He couldn't. Not while he had a shred of pride left. What would he say after today? Turning up unannounced would only make him look even more unhinged.

Gabriel headed for home.

Despite his protest this afternoon, he'd known what he was getting into with Dominic. Dominic had been clear from the start that he wasn't looking for a relationship, only sex. Gabriel had gone along with it, though he'd wanted much more than that. Every time they got together, his attraction for him intensified. Dominic was the ideal man for him. Gabriel had hoped, given time together, Dominic would come to feel the same way.

It didn't matter what Gabriel said or did — he couldn't get close to him, not emotionally. Dominic was adamant — he only wanted sex.

Until Arnie had come along.

Now he seemed to want everything.

What did Arnie have that he didn't? Gabriel stared grimly at the road as he considered the question. He was gorgeous, successful, rich. He still had a full head of hair, which was more than Gabriel did. The widow's peak he'd developed in the last couple of years was advancing fast. He'd have to consider a hair transplant soon if he was going to halt the course of nature.

There were no such worries for Arnie. He was perfect. *He always has been.*

Gabriel should know. He'd had a painful, unrequited crush on him the whole time they were growing up. He couldn't blame Dominic for falling in love with Arnie when he'd been there himself.

He sighed. He could agonize about this for days and weeks to come, or he could get over it and move on.

Let's see how I feel in the morning.

Emotionally, he was already in a better place than before. A good night's sleep might resolve everything.

Gabriel parked in front of his house. There were a handful of lights still on in the neighboring houses, but most people would be in bed. Which was exactly where he wanted to be. He'd have one drink just to take the edge of things then head up.

He unlocked the front door and stepped into the hall to switch off the burglar alarm.

As he did, a dark figure came up so fast behind him that Gabriel did not notice until it was too late.

A knife was thrust into his back. So sharp that at first all he felt was a dull pressure.

It was only when the blade was withdrawn and shoved into him a second time that the pain began.

Chapter Sixteen

Arnie watched Dominic get out of bed and walk to the window, taking pleasure in the bounce of his big arse as he crossed the room. Dominic opened the curtains and drew up the blinds, revealing another perfect summer morning. His powerful, naked body stood bathed in sunlight. As he gazed out of the window, Arnie snuggled into the pillow and enjoyed the view from the bed.

Dominic had all the attributes he found attractive in a man — muscle, strength, body hair. Naturally masculine. *And what stamina.* They had made love four times during the night and when he woke up, Arnie had still felt the pressure of a solid morning erection against his back.

This was all new. Waking in someone else's bed. Not a hotel — he was used to those — but somebody's own bed, in a room full of their personal stuff. There was a leather reading chair in the corner — Dominic had draped his clothes across it when they had come to bed. A tall dresser against the far wall. The floor was dark oak and the ceiling beams had been exposed, treated and varnished in a color to match. There was dark paper on the wall behind the bed, while the other three walls were painted ivory. It was the kind of room an interior designer would charge a fortune for, but Arnie knew without asking that Dominic had done all the work himself. It suited his personality so well.

"What time is it?" Arnie asked, still focused on the high muscular peaks of Dominic's butt.

"Nearly eight. What time do you have to collect AJ?"

"Not till later. Why, you're not kicking me out, are you?"

Dominic turned. "As if. I want to keep you here for as long as I can." He came back to the bed, his semi-hard cock swinging from side to side, before sliding under the covers.

Arnie reached across and slipped his arms around him, needing skin to skin contact.

"This is nice," he said. "Waking up beside you." He moved his hand along Dominic's flank, from his chest all to the way to his waist. After a long night of sex, there was still so much of this body he wanted to explore.

Dominic murmured agreement. In the natural light of morning, Arnie saw more clearly the tints of amber and gold in his brown eyes. His beard had grown a little overnight and, with his less than perfect morning hair, it gave him a sexy, disheveled appearance, which made him even more attractive.

They were comfortable seeing each other like this, ungroomed and unstyled.

An unexpected question popped into Arnie's mind. *Had Gabriel ever stayed over like this? Had he enjoyed early mornings in this bed too?* From what Dominic said, it seemed unlikely. *Does it matter? That was before we ever met.* Dominic had a past. They both did. They were adults with a fair amount of history between them. Arnie shoved the thoughts of Gabriel aside. It wasn't the time. There was a conversation he'd have to have with Gabriel at some point, for the sake of their friendship, but he didn't have to think about it now. Everything could wait.

Dominic had noticed the change in his manner. "You look troubled," he said. "Anything wrong?"

"Not at all," Arnie smiled. "Far from it. Right now, everything is perfect."

Dominic shuffled closer, entwining their legs. "If you're worried about what happens next, you shouldn't be."

"Worried is the wrong word. I know what I want to happen."

"Good. Because I want to continue what we're doing. I want you. I want to get to know you properly. You and your family. AJ. We have other people to consider, circumstances beyond our control — I'm aware of all of that. Believe me when I tell you this — I'm prepared to wait. I'll give you all the time and space you need. As long you feel the same, the waiting will be worth it."

"That's just it," Arnie sighed. "I don't want to wait. I want you now. I want this now." He patted the bed, then waved his arm around the room. "You know I've never had a boyfriend. Not a real one. There've been affairs and casual relationships, similar to what you had with Gabriel. All on the quiet with no chance of anything meaningful developing. You're the first man I've met who makes me want more. I want to take it further. Go on dates to restaurants and movies. I want you to come with us when I take AJ to the beach or for a burger."

"I'll give you all of that," Dominic said. "You only have to ask." He leaned over and kissed the tip of his nose. "And there are no skeletons in my closest. There's nothing bad that's going to come out and bite you in the press. I work, I write, I mess around with boats — that's all there is to me."

"There's a *lot* more to you than that. You proved it more than enough last night."

He grinned. "What I'm saying is, don't worry about me. Do what you have to do for the sake of your boy, and I'll be here for you when you're ready."

"You're too good to be true," Arnie said, moving his hand to Dominic's butt.

"I hate to tell you this, but you're gonna have to lay off that." He wriggled his arse for emphasis. "For this morning at least. I am sore as hell after last night."

"Sorry," Arnie said, moving his hand away.

"There's nothing to be sorry about." He laughed. "I'm just not that used to it, that's all. Especially to someone as big as you."

Now Arnie laughed. "To be honest, I feel the same way too. Last night I couldn't get enough, but this morning my butthole is saying *what the hell were you thinking*."

They rolled onto their backs, side by side, and gazed at the ceiling. *This is enough*, Arnie thought. The sex had been incredible, but there was something more extraordinary about lying naked next to another man and being one hundred percent comfortable with him.

"I've got an idea," Dominic said. "Though you may think it's too soon."

"Tell me."

"You could bring AJ by the station later. I'm going in this afternoon to do some maintenance on the boat. Why not drop by? I'll show him around and let him sit at the wheel. I'm sure he'll enjoy it. Most young lads do. And it'll allow him to get to know me. Then it won't be such a shock when he finds out we're seeing each other. Unless he hates me, of course. In that case, this plan could be an utter fail."

"AJ won't hate you. He's a good judge of character. Just like his dad."

As he thought about it, Arnie realized it wasn't a bad idea. AJ was already interested in the lifeboat. Before they'd even come this summer, he'd asked if his granddad could arrange a similar kind of thing. It had all been so hectic that until now there hadn't been an opportunity. And Dominic was right. It would allow them to get to know each other better before dropping the bombshell on the boy.

Arnie rolled over, swinging his leg across Dominic's body, to sit up and straddle him. Dominic's eyes widened in surprise.

"All right," Arnie said. "You're on. I'll ask him, and if he's interested, I'll bring him along after lunch."

Arnie ground his hips, letting the weight of his balls fall on Dominic's stomach. His cock hardened.

"What's this?" Dominic asked, wrapping his fingers around the stiff flesh.

"I reckon I've got about three hours before I have to think about being a dad again. Our arses may need a rest after last night, but my mouth and hands are good to go."

Dominic threw back his head and laughed loudly. "Then we should make good use of the time. Let's get to it, Daddy."

* * * *

Cyrus answered the door when Arnie arrived to collect AJ. His brother-in-law did not try to hide his contempt. "They're through there," he said, turning his back and heading upstairs. Off to his study, Arnie guessed, where he'd work all day, even though it was the weekend.

He'd given up caring what Cyrus' problem was. Homophobia or jealousy — he couldn't decide. It was Cyrus' issue. If they could get through the rest of their lives, barely talking, faking civility for the sake of his sister, that was good enough for Arnie. He didn't care for the man Cyrus had turned into. *Let him rot in his own poison if that's what he wants.*

He followed the sound of excited squeals and shouting to the back of the house. AJ was in the garden with his cousins and the dog. Sophie sat in the conservatory with her iPad and a tray of coffee, keeping an eye on the kids through the open doors.

"Morning," Arnie said.

Sophie put down the tablet and took off her glasses. "Good morning." She smirked. "And how was last night? From the look on your face, I'd say you enjoyed yourself."

"Whatever happened to discretion?"

"Between siblings? There's no such thing and there never was. Tell me all about it."

"No way. You'll blab to our mam and then it'll be all over town by this evening."

Sophie's eyes widened in delight. "So there is something to tell. Come on, spill."

"Thanks for babysitting," he said, changing the subject. "Everything go all right?"

"They're all still in one piece, as you can see." She gestured outside. "No disasters. So, come on, you can at least tell me if you're going to see him again."

"Who?"

"Dominic Melton."

"Who's he?" he asked nonchalantly.

"You're cruising for a bruising, big brother."

"Look, I don't want to make a fuss, and I don't want everyone gossiping. It's early days. *Very* early. Can we just let things be and see what happens?"

Sophie poured him a cup of coffee. "You're being cautious, and I know why. Your skanky ex is all over the morning news again today. Tara was a mistake. If it wasn't for AJ, I'd say she was the biggest mistake you ever made. But Dominic is nothing like her. He's perfect for you. I've thought so for ages. Long before I heard a whisper that you might be into him. Go for it. You won't regret it this time."

"We'll see."

"I'm right. I'm telling you. And if you don't go for him, then I might just trade in Cyrus and steal him out from under you. Half the town will be green with envy when they hear about this. And the other half will be jealous of Dominic."

"Let's make sure they don't hear about it for a while, eh? I'm serious. Let's have some privacy while we figure things out."

"I'll keep quiet on one condition," she said.

"Which is?"

"You grab this chance of happiness with both hands and hold on as tight as you can. You deserve it, Arnie. I mean it. I really want to see you happy, and I'm certain he's the man who can do it."

* * * *

AJ's eyes widened in delight when Arnie suggested he could look around the lifeboat station and maybe get onboard the boat.

"Can I go out to sea?" he asked.

"No, not today. But you can sit in the driver's seat and see how everything works."

"Cool."

Arnie drove him straight from Sophie's into the town center. Sophie had said the kids had been up since six thirty and had their breakfast by seven. AJ claimed he was starving when they left the house. He took him to a small café on a side street just off the waterfront. Because of the location, it was popular with local people but less so with the tourists, which meant they should be left alone. AJ ordered a ham and cheese sandwich with a bowl of fries and a diet cola. Arnie, who'd had bacon sandwiches with Dominic a little over an hour earlier, asked for a pot of breakfast tea.

"Can we go on a boat sometime?" AJ asked.

"If that's want you want, sure. They run trips along the coast from here in the marina. We can go one day this week if the weather holds."

"Will we see sharks? Or killer whales?"

Typical AJ. The boy was always thinking about fearsome creatures. "I don't think so, son. We don't get many of them around here. There's nothing to be scared of in the sea at North Point."

"I'm not scared. I just want to see a big shark. Like Meg."

"Who's Meg?"

"She's a giant shark," he said as though it was the most obvious thing in the world. "We watched the movie last night. *The Meg*. It's like a giant dinosaur shark. It was so cool."

That explained the sudden interest. "Well, I don't think we have ordinary sharks around here, let along monster ones, so we can relax on that front."

Once finished, they left the car where it was and walked to the lifeboat station. As they passed The Lobster Pot, he saw a member of Gabriel's team setting tables out front. There was a discussion he'd have to have sometime, but not today. He didn't want to spoil what had been a nice morning by starting an argument with Gabriel. Hopefully it wouldn't come to that. Gabriel can't have meant what he'd said to Dominic about going to the press. It was out of character. He wasn't that petty — Arnie was sure of it.

He would ask his parents to look after AJ for a couple of hours on Monday and arrange to meet Gabriel for a coffee somewhere. This could all be straightened out. Neither of them had to make things difficult.

Dominic was already at the station when they arrived. The front doors were open and Noel was sweeping the path in front with a long-handled broom. Although it was less than two hours since he'd seen him last, Dominic was a feast for the eyes. He wore a pair of nicely fitting jeans and the customary navy polo shirt. He'd showered and trimmed his beard, and his hair was combed into its usual neat style. *Very nice.*

"Hello," he said, smiling, friendly and not over-familiar.

"Hi," Arnie said, as though they only knew each other in passing.

"You must be AJ," Dominic said. "I'm Dominic and this is Noel — we both help around here."

Noel gave a curt nod before getting on with the brushing. AJ glanced from Dominic to the boat behind him in the station. "Can I really have a look around?"

"Of course you can, come on. It's this way."

Arnie followed and was soon ignored as AJ became enthralled with Dominic and the lifeboat. It surprised him to see that Dominic had such an easygoing manner with children, considering he had no close family of his own. Then again, hadn't he said they often welcomed schools and youth groups for tours around the station and to educate them on water safety? He was a natural.

He helped AJ onto the boat and followed him in.

"Are you the captain?" AJ asked.

"I'm the helmsman," Dominic said.

"What does that mean?"

"I drive the boat. Come along here and I'll show you where I sit."

He let AJ take the seat in the stern beside the engine and hold the wheel. "Where does the captain sit?"

"We don't have a captain. Our boat isn't big enough to need one. We're all a team with different jobs to do."

"If you do the driving, you must be the closest thing to a captain, mustn't you?"

Arnie was pleased to see AJ getting on so well with him, too. AJ didn't know the real reason behind this, but it was a start, to see if they had a connection. If AJ had acted like a brat or given Dominic attitude, they'd have a challenge in their hands going forward, but the way they were behaving, everything looked good.

Maybe I can have this. It seemed too much to hope for. For the longest time, Arnie had ruled out the possibility of a relationship. Since taking full charge of AJ, he'd put his own desires on hold and hadn't dared consider it. He supposed things were different now. AJ was older.

He would soon be ten. And while Tara might be acting up, things were pretty settled elsewhere. AJ was happy at school and at home. There were no tantrums or hissy fits. He was a good kid.

There'd never been a better time for Arnie to consider the real possibility of having a boyfriend.

That was all it would be for now. A consideration. This was a very tiny step in the right direction. Not even a step—just a toe over the line. There was such a long way to go.

It's a start, at least.

"Have you seen any sharks when you've been out in this?" AJ asked.

"Sure," Dominic said. "Sometimes big ones."

"*See*," AJ hollered at Arnie. "I told you there were sharks."

"I'm not sure that's helping," Arnie said to Dominic.

Dominic winked in response and continued the tour.

Afterward, while AJ was in the main station with Noel, looking at models of previous lifeboats, Arnie and Dominic went to the kitchen to fetch them drinks.

"That went well," Dominic said. "Don't you think?"

"I think it did," Arnie said, sliding up to cop a feel of Dominic's butt and plant a kiss on his cheek. "Thank you. He likes you, I can tell."

"I like him," Dominic said, pulling Arnie in for a proper embrace. "He's a nice kid with a genuine interest. You should see some of the little shits we get coming through here. They couldn't give a toss about the boat or what we do. We're just an inconvenience when they'd rather be playing on their phones. AJ didn't look at his phone once."

"That's because he doesn't have one. He has a tablet for playing games, but it stays at home. I don't allow him to bring it out with us."

Dominic raised his eyebrows. "That must make you *very* popular."

"I'll keep it up as long as I can. I'll have to give in eventually, in another year or two, but for now, I want him to enjoy being a boy. There's plenty of time ahead for him to grow up. I'm glad he's still into dinosaurs and monsters. I was the same at that age."

"There's something we have in common. I was too." Dominic put his arms around Arnie, pulling him into a loose embrace. "It feels good, doesn't it? All this? Meeting AJ?"

Arnie kissed him on the mouth. "It does. Better than I ever imagined."

It was true. Following the stresses of the last few weeks, allowing himself to lower his guard and fall in love was the last thing he'd expected. Things were looking up. He hoped they'd stay that way.

Chapter Seventeen

"Can we go for a walk on the beach?" AJ asked.

They had just come out of the lifeboat station and Arnie was about to head toward where he'd left the car. The good weather of the morning was on the turn, with rapidly developing clouds coming in on a stiff breeze from the sea. The temperature had dropped several degrees since their arrival but was still pleasantly warm in the marina.

"I thought you wanted to watch a movie this afternoon," he said.

"No. I want to see the caves under the point."

"The what?"

"The caves under the point. I heard they go right beneath the house we're living in. There are tunnels where smugglers and Vikings used to hide their loot and treasure."

Arnie tried not to laugh. "Who told you that?"

"*Everyone* says it."

"Everyone, eh? There are some small caves along the coast, but not the kind you're thinking of. Just little recesses where the sea has cut into the rock. No tunnels."

AJ didn't believe his old man. "Can we go for a look, anyway? Please."

"Sure we can. Don't get your hopes up too high, that's all I'm saying." He took AJ's hand. "Come on, we need to cross the bridge first."

They went over to the north side of the river and followed the harbor wall until they reached the path that led to the beach below North Point. The beach was quiet for a Saturday afternoon. Arnie expected there to be more people around, but as they walked down to the shore, he realized how cool the sea wind was. A decent-sized swell was throwing up some big waves, but there weren't any surfers around to enjoy it.

"Did you have fun with the lifeboat?" he asked, as they headed north along the beach.

AJ was excited and Arnie had to step up to keep pace with the little guy.

"It was cool. Did Grandad used to be a lifeboat man?"

"He did, yes. Not in that boat, though. It's fairly new, but he used to go out on rescues all the time when I was your age."

"Why aren't you in the crew?" AJ asked, with a fair whiff of judgement.

"I don't have the sea legs for it. Besides, you have to live here all the time if you want to be in the crew. You need to be ready to launch the boat as soon as they raise the alarm. I could hardly do that from London, could I?"

"I guess not," AJ said grudgingly. "It would take way too long." He seemed to give this some more thought before asking, "Why don't we live here? Gran and Grandad are here. And Conner and Indina. Why can't we live with them?"

Arnie looked at him thoughtfully. "Would you like that?"

"Of course. It's so much better than London."

"Really? What do you like so much?"

"I already told you. Everyone's here, except us. And we don't have a beach in London, or a lifeboat, or a dog."

It surprised him to hear AJ talk like this. The boy had always enjoyed their visits to Nyemouth but had never expressed a longing to live here. "You'd have to change schools," he pointed out.

"That's all right. Conner says I could go to school with him."

So *that* was it. The sleepover with his cousins has put this idea in his head. Arnie could imagine all three of them, sitting up later than they were allowed, whispering in the dark about the things they would do together.

"It's not that simple, son," he said. "We can't move as easily as that."

"Why not? I could go to school with Conner and you could join the lifeboat crew."

He laughed. "I can't join just like that. It takes a lot of training."

"Dominic will show you what to do. He knows everything."

Arnie looked at his son. Was there a hidden intention behind that statement? Or was it as innocent as it appeared? Had the little tykes discussed *him* during their sleepover? After AJ's earlier comments about him getting a boyfriend, he wouldn't put anything past him. The boy was wiser than he gave him credit for, and growing up fast.

And just as he was thinking his son was older than his years, AJ said, "Noel saw a shark off the point last summer. He told me this afternoon."

"He did, did he?"

AJ nodded vigorously and gazed out to sea, hopefully searching for a huge beast. "He said if you keep your eyes on the sea, you never know what might be out there. We might see a Meg, like in the movie."

"I don't know about that, but he's right about the sea. You can see all sorts of things in the water."

"How far to the smugglers' caves?"

"I told you there aren't any." They had reached a point where the sandstone rocks jutted out from the base of the cliffs. They had to walk farther down the beach, closer to the water, to maneuver around them. "I think we should turn back now. It's getting colder."

He hadn't been keeping an eye on the tide either. Was it on the way out or coming in?

"Let's go a bit farther. Until we find the first cave. *Please*."

"Five more minutes, then we're going home. Cave or no cave, okay?"

Arnie's phone sounded an alert as they walked around the rocks. A news update. He'd set it to notify him whenever there was fresh info on Sandy Costello. He tapped straight to the website of the local newspaper. *North Point Victim Comes Out of Coma*, read the top story, *Sandy Costello Awake*.

"Thank God." Arnie exhaled relief and scrolled through the page to read further. According to the site, Sandy had pulled around sometime on Friday afternoon. They had moved her out of the intensive care unit to a specialist spinal injury ward. Her troubles were far from over, but she was conscious. Her situation sounded so much better than it had before, though there was little information. He went to another site, but the details were much the same. If she was out of intensive care, that had to mean she was stable. Was she talking? Could she remember what happened?

Could she identify her attacker?

Not likely, he guessed, considering the speed with which it had happened. And with the disguise her assailant had worn, it would have to be someone she knew intimately well for her to recognize them.

Arnie had to meet her. Not today. It was far too soon, but he'd contact the hospital when they got home, find out when they expected her to be well enough to receive visitors. Though they didn't know each other, they had a connection now, something that would likely bond them for the rest of their lives.

A short wave lapped across Arnie's feet. It startled him and brought him back to the moment. He watched the white foam retreat down the beach, before another came rushing forward. He stepped quickly out of the way.

That answered his earlier query.

The tide was coming in.

"AJ, it's time to go."

Looking up, he saw the boy had wandered ahead, darting in and out of the rock face in search of the mythical caves.

"Hey, AJ," he called. "The tide is on the turn. We have to go back."

"I think we're nearly there," his son called. "It can't be much farther."

"We have to go now," he said with authority. "Come on, let's go."

Another wave washed up to his feet, and he took a bigger a step backward. He'd forgotten how fast the tides turned up here in the point.

"Come on now," he shouted, anger creeping into his voice. He shouldn't take it out on the boy. It was his fault they'd come this way without checking the tides, but there was no time to mess about. They had to turn straight back before the route to the town was blocked by the sea.

AJ trudged reluctantly toward him, his bottom lip sticking out. "It's not fair."

"We'll come back tomorrow," Arnie said kindly. "Nice and early, so we have plenty of time. Okay? The tide is against us today."

Suddenly AJ looked up, surprised, gazing at something over Arnie's shoulder.

"What are *you* doing here?" AJ asked.

"Huh?"

Arnie turned to see who he was taking to. Before he could complete the maneuver, he was struck hard on the back of the head by a blunt object. The impact was sickening, as reverberations juddered through his skull. Blunt pain became blinding. *What just happened?*

Something hit him a second time in almost the same place as before. Colors and lights exploded before his eyes, which quickly dimmed to darkness.

"*Dad,*" AJ screamed as he watched his father fall to the sand unconscious. As he rushed forward to help, the figure dressed entirely in black raised the rock threateningly toward him. AJ shrank against the raggedy cliff-face.

"Stay where you are, kid, or you're next."

Tears sprang into the boy's eyes and spilled down his cheeks.

Noel Garrard, who he had last seen in the lifeboat station less than an hour ago, glared menacingly. When he had appeared just a moment ago, AJ had thought he'd come to show him the way to the smuggler's caves. His face looked so different from the friendly boy who'd shown him around the boat and told him about the shark he'd seen off the point last summer. That Noel had been cool, with his knowledge of the sea and its creatures. This Noel was horrible. His features were twisted and ugly, and he looked old and cruel as his lips drew back from his teeth in a sneer. He reminded AJ of the nasty dog that barked at all the kids when they passed its house, on the way to school. The dog would stick his head through the gate, looking for an opportunity to savage any passerby.

There was a huge rock in Noel's hand — it filled his entire fist. The rock he'd smashed over Arnie's head. Taking him from behind and striking without warning. There were red streaks on the jagged sandstone. Blood.

Dad's blood.

Noel bent and picked up Arnie's phone, which he'd dropped as he fell. He glanced briefly at the screen, then back to AJ, before smiling and casting the phone into the sea. AJ watched it tumble through the air before disappearing into the waves.

Noel looked at AJ and raised the rock threateningly. With tears pouring down his face, AJ flinched and dropped to his haunches.

"Please don't," he cried.

Noel laughed, a mocking sound, and lunged at him again. AJ screamed and leaped out of his reach.

"Stop it."

With a sneer, Noel stepped away. He tossed the rock at Arnie, striking a blow between his shoulders. Arnie was out of it and didn't respond.

"See you, kid." Noel's voice and face were full of scorn. "There's no fun in smashing both your brains in. I'll let the sea do the rest of the dirty work."

With a final laugh, Noel spun around and ran, pelting through water that came up to his knees to make it back to the beach.

Terrified but aware of the danger they were in, AJ hurried to his father. Arnie lay facedown on the sand. Before AJ could shake him for a response, a large wave rushed over him, covering Arnie completely for one awful moment before retreating.

It was the coldest thing AJ had ever experienced.

"Dad," he shouted, shaking his shoulder. "Dad, please wake up. Please."

Arnie was unresponsive.

Another wave washed over him, smaller than the first but just as scary.

The tide was coming in.

Looking in the direction Noel had run, he saw the route back to the main beach was already cut off. In a few more minutes, the spot where he stood would also be underwater.

Cold, wet and with a deepening sense of despair, AJ tried to wake his unconscious father.

Chapter Eighteen

Noel Garrard raced across the path to the peak of North Point, a steep ascent over uneven ground. By the time he reached the top, his breath rasped so hard his throat was sore. He had to calm down – he didn't want anyone to see him and pay attention to his unusual behavior. *No chance of that*, he thought, looking around. The point was deserted. The wind was stronger here than it had been on the beach. Colder and more biting. The conditions were worsening quickly and there were no tourists or locals about.

His pushed onward. He didn't want to miss the moment the tide came rushing in to carry away the shitty kid and his faggot dad. It may already be too late. He'd only made it to the safety of the beach himself when the sea cut off the route behind. Another minute and he would have been floundering down there with them.

Except you're not. He giggled. The look on the kid's face had been priceless. The utter disbelief and fear he'd shown when threatened with the rock. It was almost as good as the look in that stupid bitch's eyes when he'd thrown her over the edge a couple of weeks back. Nothing could top that—the split second when comprehension had dawned on her, when she'd realized what he was doing.

Would he ever experience anything as good as that again? It seemed unlikely.

Still, this was better than nothing.

He remembered the impact of the rock as it hit Arnie Walker's skull, the way it had jarred his wrist and resounded through every part of Noel's body. Instant hard-on. He was no fag, not like Walker, but something about violence aroused Noel far more than any sexual experience.

The power of taking a life. Of becoming God.

That was the best.

Noel hurried along the point, passing the house where Arnie and the boy had been staying, making sure he kept well out of the range of their CCTV cameras. It wouldn't do to get caught on film at the exact moment the tenants were washed out to sea. Once they realized the kid and his dad were missing, someone was bound to check every frame of footage, looking for a clue to their disappearance. Noel Garrard wouldn't be snared so easily.

No, they would never catch him.

Noel was too clever for that. Too wily and smart.

He reached the area where he knew he'd find them and approached the cliff edge with caution. He got on his hands and knees, inching forward through the grass and mud, until he could look right over. The tide had claimed the sandy beach. Ferocious waves battered the rocks, throwing huge white spumes into the air. He was too late. The sea must have taken them already. *Fuck.*

He scanned the heaving waves for a sign of them. A head bobbing above the water. A corpse lying facedown in the surf. Nothing.

Then he saw movement, directly below. On the rocks. Noel leaned farther over for a better look.

The clever little cunt.

They were directly beneath him. Somehow the boy had dragged his father above the tide line. For now, at least. The waves were coming closer and soon the spot where they lay would be under water. How the hell had he done it? How had a puny kid managed to the shift the weight of a large, unconscious man and drag him to temporary safety? Arnie Walker must be a solid weight at the best of times, let alone when he was wet and out for the count.

The kid had him on his back and looked like he was trying to revive him, shaking his shoulders and crying.

The resentment was crippling. They should have been carried away on the tide by now. Noel gnashed his teeth together, his breath rasping with frustration. What if the man came around?

It won't do them any good, he told himself. He'd thrown Arnie's phone into the sea. They had no means of raising the alarm. And no one would hear their cries. The winds were too strong, and with a storm forecast for tonight, the fishing fleet had returned early. There was no chance of an offshore vessel spotting them and radioing the Coastguard for help.

Calm down. It won't be long. They'll be dead soon. And you'll see it. At last, you'll see.

As he watched, a big wave broke over the rocks, drenching the boy and his father. Not powerful enough to wash them off. Not yet.

The swell deepened and the force of the waves grew stronger with every second.

Noel settled down to watch the proceedings. Things hadn't gone exactly to plan so far. But surely it was better this way. The boy's terror must be off the scale by now, knowing he was about to die and there was no one, not even his daddy, who could save him.

Noel bit his top lip and waited for the wave which would take them away.

* * * *

When he got home from the lifeboat station, Dominic took Brandy for a walk. It was earlier than the dog was used to, but it was shaping up for a nasty afternoon. If he took her for a good walk now, she'd be content to do her business in the garden later. He pulled on his waterproof jacket and took her out on South Point. Brandy lacked enthusiasm and the strengthening wind meant she wanted to turn for home as soon as she'd relieved herself. Dominic didn't try to dissuade her. The conditions were turning filthy. Tea and maybe a plate of toast were the perfect remedies for such a bleak afternoon.

In the house, he turned on the lamps in the living room and put the kettle on to boil.

It was a shame he couldn't look forward to another evening with Arnie. Last night had gone so fast. With a little luck, they could repeat it soon. The boy had seemed friendly enough this afternoon. Maybe he could take them both out for burgers or a pizza sometime soon. Father and son. *Why not?* Just because he had given little thought to children in the past, there was no reason why he couldn't do it now. He didn't dislike kids. Other than the groups who came through the lifeboat station, he had no real experience of them. They weren't something he'd expected to be part of his life. He'd had no urge to be a father himself.

He would have to change that way of thinking if he was going to be with Arnie. Arnie and AJ came as a package and he could not have one without the other.

The idea would take some getting used to.

As the kettle boiled and he made a pot of tea, Dominic decided that if there was no Arnie tonight, he'd settle for the next best thing and find one of his movies or TV shows on Netflix. He sat at the kitchen table, waiting for the tea to brew, and browsed the available titles on his tablet. He'd barely got started when there was an urgent knock at the front door.

Jacob entered without waiting. His overcoat and hat were soaked. As he took them off in the hall, Dominic saw the lines of concern drawn across his face. Jacob hurried through to the kitchen.

"Is something wrong?" Dominic asked. The old man did not look good. His skin was pasty and there was a noticeable tremor in his hands. "Sit down."

Dominic helped him to a seat and poured a hot cup of tea, adding a heaped spoonful of sugar and a generous glug of milk, just how Jacob liked it. The cup trembled in his hands as Jacob took a sip.

"Are you unwell?" Dominic asked, putting a hand on his forehead. His skin was cold. "Should I call a doctor?"

"No. No, I'm fine. It's not me. From the way you're behaving, I take it you haven't heard the news?"

"What news?"

Jacob took another sip of tea and seemed to steel himself, sitting straighter in the chair, before saying, "Gabriel. He's dead."

Dominic heard the words but not their meaning. It took time for what Jacob had said to register. "Gabriel? No. There must be a mistake."

"There's not," Jacob countered. "I was in the town talking to young Cheryl Bratton when we heard. Cheryl has a Saturday job waiting tables at The Lobster Pot. I was there when everyone found out."

It had the unnatural, distant impression of a dream. *Gabriel. Dead. Impossible.* Dominic waited for the world to snap back into focus. When it didn't, he asked, "What happened?"

Jacob stood and poured another cup of tea. He set it in front of Dominic. "Drink this. If you need something stronger, I'll get it for you afterward."

"After what? Jacob, what the hell is going on? Tell me what you know."

Jacob sat down with a sigh. "Dominic, Gabriel has been murdered."

Dominic stared at him, open-mouthed. "What? How?"

"He didn't turn up for work this morning, but that wasn't so unusual. Apparently, he'd often let the manager open on Saturday, then Gabriel would come in later and stay until closing. They said it was rare for him not to be there by one. The staff needed some key that only Gabriel has to access to, so they started calling him. When they didn't get an answer, the manager, a woman called Jenny, drove over to the house to collect it. She found him in the hall. There was blood everywhere. She said it looked like someone had stabbed him several times. I understand she tried to revive him, but it was hopeless. It must have happened sometime last night and there was nothing she could do by then."

Dominic heard every word Jacob said, but the disconnection from reality continued. Gabriel murdered. Stabbed to death in his own home. It made no sense. Gabriel didn't have any enemies. He was well-liked, a popular figure in the local community. There could be no motive to kill him. And yet, he considered everything else happening in Nyemouth right now—the attempted murder of Sandy Costello, and hadn't someone been stalking Arnie all week? The hooded figure on the CCTV footage. *The same guy who attacked Sandy?* Could Gabriel's murder be connected to that? No. That was insane. Paranoid.

But murder. In a small town like this.

Gabriel is dead.

Jesus. In his previous career, Dominic had had many encounters with death. Violent and ugly, it wasn't something he ever got used to. But with experience, he'd learned how to deal with it. *All part of the deal when serving your country.*

He did not expect it in civilian life, much less happening to someone he knew well.

"Could it have been a robbery? He might have disturbed a burglar when he got home."

Jacob swallowed his tea. "Possibly. The police will consider every option. They always do. But...I don't know. It's just..."

"What?"

"With everything else that's gone on around here lately. And now this. It's...it's not right. Something doesn't feel right. I don't know. I've lived here my entire life. Nyemouth has always been a peaceful town.

It's not a violent place. And now there's been an attempted murder and an actual murder, all in the space of a couple of weeks. There's something very wrong here."

Dominic nodded grimly and agreed with every word.

* * * *

Cold rain lashed against AJ as he tried to revive Arnie. They were already soaked from the sea, which rose higher with every minute. His father showed no sign of coming around. Not one murmur or groan as AJ shook his shoulders and shouted full in his face.

"Dad. Dad, come on. Please. Wake up."

With a thunderous roar, another wave smashed against the rocks, soaking them with its spume. AJ didn't notice the cold anymore.

It was hopeless. There was no way his father was going come around. He was breathing, that was something — it meant he wasn't dead. *But he soon will be if we stay here. We both will.*

With each crashing wave the sea came higher up to the rocks.

AJ knew they had to move. There wasn't much farther they could go. Maybe another three yards from where they were to the bottom of the cliff. It was better than nothing. Arnie was a dead weight, a big man without the added burden of his water-logged clothes. AJ steadied himself. He'd done this once already, hauling his lifeless father from the sand onto the rocks to get him out of imminent danger. He could do it again.

He hunkered down beside his father's head and wriggled his arms beneath him, hooking his elbows into Arnie's armpits. There was blood in Arnie's hair, at the back of his skull. *Can't do anything about that now.* They had to escape the rising water for as long as possible. With a momentous effort, he heaved. The weight was incredible. Arnie seemed even heavier than before, but nothing could deter him. AJ wrenched again and succeeded in dragging Arnie's dead weight a couple of precious inches across the rock. With a deep breath he renewed his effort, pulling with every fiber of his being. He gained a few more inches. He could do this. Slowly, and with infinite determination, AJ dragged Arnie from the edge of the rocks to the base of the cliff.

That was it. He could go no farther.

Exhausted and out of breath, AJ knelt beside his father and lifted his head to rest it on his thighs, taking care not to put pressure on the wound. Arnie groaned.

"Dad," AJ said, hopefully. There was no further response.

AJ was on his own.

He dug into the inside pocket of his jacket and found the small mobile phone his mother had given him. She'd warned him not to tell Arnie about it. It was their secret and she would use it to stay in touch with him when they were apart. The phone hadn't rung once in the two years since Tara had given it to him, but AJ had held on to it, keeping the battery charged in the hope that his mother would call him sometime.

It was a guilty secret. His father would be mad if he found out he had it. To AJ, it was worth the risk. The phone was the only link he had back to his mother. The single thing that made him hope she still loved him. It was a secret worth keeping. And now it might save their lives.

AJ dialed 9-9-9.

"Hello, emergency," the operator answered. "Which service do you require?"

"Coastguard," he shouted. "And hurry, please. We need a lifeboat right now."

* * * *

Dominic and Jacob hadn't moved from the kitchen table. The truth about Gabriel's murder was slow to sink in. Was it only yesterday that they'd argued in the marina? It seemed like months ago. Years. And the subject of their disagreement—pure bullshit. They were grown men, adults. They should have sorted it out in a mature manner, not sniped at each other like kids and ended their relationship on a bitter note.

The last words they'd said to each other had been spoken in pointless anger.

Rain lashed against the window. The change in weather seemed appropriate, given the sudden shift in circumstances.

"Do you think anyone has told Arnie?" he asked.

Jacob looked up, surprised. Dominic's voice dragging him back to reality. "I don't know."

"They were friends. Best friends when they were kids."

"It won't take long for the news to spread. There were enough people around when I heard about it. It will be all over town by now."

"He shouldn't hear it through gossip." Dominic retrieved his phone. Arnie had said he was going to spend the afternoon with AJ. With the boy to distract him, he might not have heard yet. He dialed his number and waited. It went to voicemail. *Damn.* Dominic left a message asking him to call as soon as he could. He didn't mention what had happened to Gabriel.

"With any luck, Martin or Elizabeth will get to him first and he won't hear it second-hand," Jacob said.

"I still can't believe it," Dominic said. "We're sitting here talking about it, but none of it seems real. How could anyone kill him? And in such a brutal way."

"Maybe it's what you said before. He disturbed an intruder. Who knows what goes through the minds of some people? If they're desperate enough to commit burglary, they could be capable of anything."

"Gabriel was a fit guy. Healthy and strong. Most opportunistic thieves would run away from a man like that. Not stab him to death. *Bastards.*"

They sat quietly for a few moments, with just the drumming of the rain on the window to disturb the silence.

Suddenly Dominic's lifeboat pager, which was clipped to his belt, went off.

Both men leapt to attention, all personal concerns forgotten in that moment.

"Shit," Jacob said, "What an awful day for a callout."

Dominic rushed to the front door, grabbing his jacket. "Will you see to the dog and lock up for me?"

Jacob was already on his feet. "Go," he said. "Don't worry about this. I'll sort it. I'll see you down there."

Without another word, Dominic ran out of the house and pelted down the rain-soaked road to the station.

Chapter Nineteen

Dominic was the first of the crew to arrive at the station. He came in through the side entrance and quickly unlocked the folding front doors, drawing them back ready to launch. He was pulling on his safety suit when four more volunteers arrived.

"You two get suited up," he shouted at Haig and Minty, the most experienced of the team. In horrific conditions such as this, he wanted the very best men in the boat with him. He trusted the others to prep the tractor.

Dominic climbed straight onboard and radioed to the Coastguard that they would launch any minute. "What do we know so far?" he asked.

"Two casualties at the foot of the cliff on North Point. A father and son. The man is unconscious. The boy is uninjured at present. They've been cut off by the tide."

"Any information on the father's injuries?"

"A head wound. We're awaiting further details. We have raised the helicopter. ETA twenty-five minutes."

Every second counted in a situation like this.

"How old is the boy?"

"Approximately nine years old. His name is AJ."

Dominic froze, the skin on his scalp tightened and his blood turned to ice water. *No. It can't be.*

"Details are sketchy at this point and somewhat confused. The boy claims he and his father were attacked on the beach. He's in a distressed state, so I'm not sure what we can believe."

"Let's get moving," Dominic shouted at the crew. "*Now.*"

Haig and Minty climbed into the boat and the tractor lowered them to the water. Dominic opened the engines and shot across the harbor.

He had to stay calm and detached from all personal concerns. It was the only way. Keep it professional and treat this like any other rescue. He couldn't allow his emotions to influence his decision-making. It would be fatal for everyone if he did.

Arnie and AJ were depending on him. He wouldn't let them down.

As soon as they left the protection of the marina, they were hit by the full force of the wind and sea. The lifeboat rode the crest of a huge wave before dropping down the other side. Dominic's stomach plunged with the sickening decent. Despite the urgency, he had to ease back on the throttle. The boat would overturn if he wasn't careful in these conditions.

He steered north, already scanning the shore and the towering cliffs.

Jesus, the way the waves were breaking on the rocks was terrifying.

Arnie and AJ had no chance out there.

Get your shit together. You'll find them. You must.

* * * *

His hearing was the first of Arnie's senses to return. A thundering sound, deep and booming, seemed to reverberate through him. Then pain, pain more intense than anything he'd ever known, like a metal shard had been shoved through the back of his skull and worked deep into his head. The next thing he felt was cold, so bitter it went down to the marrow.

Where was he? His thoughts were confused. He struggled to remember. Breakfast this morning. Yes, with Dominic. Then collecting AJ, taking him to the station and a walk on the beach.

"Help." A desperate cry. Close. Very close.

AJ.

Arnie forced his eyes open and saw his son. The dull gray light hurt his eyes. He fought through it. He was on his back, lying on something cold, hard and wet, his head in AJ's lap. As he struggled to make sense of what was happening, a wave washed over him. The saltwater stung and blurred his vision. The shock snapped him back to the present.

They were in trouble.

"AJ," he said, struggling to rise.

"Dad. Oh, thank God. You're alive. *You're alive.*" Relief was clear in AJ's voice. It pierced Arnie to the core.

He struggled into a sitting position. It took only a second to realize where they were and the direness of the situation. The sea was mountainous, ever moving and shifting, and the rocks where they lay were barely more than a foot above the water level. One strong wave would take them.

"I called for the lifeboat," AJ said. "It's on the way but I can't see it yet."

"Good boy," Arnie said, getting to his feet and leaning against the cliff face. He pulled AJ tight to him. He couldn't remember how they'd got here and his head hurt like hell, but he knew with certainty that the only reason he was alive was because of his son. Now he'd use every reserve that remained to protect the boy. "Are you hurt?"

"No, I'm fine. But the water, it keeps coming higher. If the lifeboat doesn't get here soon, we'll have nothing left to stand on."

Arnie looked up at the cliff. It stretched more than a hundred feet above them, completely sheer, its surfaced polished by centuries of sea erosion. There was no chance of climbing it.

"How long since you called the Coastguard?"

"I don't know. Ten minutes. I've no idea how long we've been here. Dad, it was Noel. He came up behind us and hit you on the head with a big stone."

"Don't worry about that now," Arnie said. Ten minutes. The lifeboat would have launched by now. Help would be on the way. He didn't know what good it would do. They were in a treacherous position, surrounded by jagged rocks and high waves. The boat wouldn't get close enough to take them off.

A surge of water rushed around their feet, cold and biting. Thankfully, it retreated over the rocks.

Arnie pulled AJ closer. The boy shivered in his arms. Hypothermia would set in if they weren't rescued soon. He picked him up. "Wrap your arms and legs around me," he instructed. "Warm yourself against me." They were both cold to the touch. AJ trembled and his teeth chattered close to Arnie's ear. He hugged his son tighter, desperate to impart all the body heat he could.

"Where is the lifeboat?" AJ asked.

The question was heart-wrenching. "Soon, son. It'll be here soon."

Arnie offered a silent prayer, begging God to make it true.

* * * *

Arnie Walker was awake. The bastard had pulled around.

Noel smashed his clenched fists against the sandstone cliff, scraping the skin and drawing blood. *How the fuck could that happen?* He'd banged that rock so hard against his head, he shouldn't ever have recovered. Hadn't he heard the crunch of bone when he hit him? Noel was certain of it. Now the bastard was on his feet and fighting to save the shitty kid.

It wouldn't do them any good. The waves coming in now looked a good six to seven feet. The next one to hit the outcrop they were standing on would wash them out to sea. Then it would be over. If they weren't battered to pieces against the rocks, the formidable currents would drag them away. And if they weren't pulled under, the cold would take care of them. They were already soaked. The sea would soon do the rest.

Noel had nothing to worry about.

God damn it. Things never went to plan for him.

The stupid woman he'd thrown over this cliff hadn't died like she should have either. From what his gran and her old cronies had been saying this morning, the bitch had made a recovery. How could that be right? A fall from this height onto the hard rocks below should be enough to kill anyone. But no, she had clung to life and robbed him of his first kill.

Only Gabriel Mayne's murder had gone to plan. Another faggot. Too stupid to look behind him when he had opened his front door. That had been easy. *Too easy.* He hadn't even tried to plead for his life as Noel stuck the knife in again and again.

And now these bastards, refusing to play ball. Arnie Walker and his brat should have been dead already, drifting in the deep.

Noel leaned farther over the edge, desperate to see what was happening. The rock where they stood was almost submerged. It wouldn't be long. One good wave—that was all it would take. Noel's pulse raced with anticipation as he willed the tide to do its job.

* * * *

The sea washed around Arnie's ankles. He set his feet firm, determined to stay upright for as long as he could. He held AJ as clear of the water as he could, with the boy's legs wrapped around his trunk and his arms around his neck. The pain in Arnie's head was constant. Noel had hit him with real force. *The bastard.* Arnie ignored it as much as possible. If he could still draw breath, he would fight to save his son.

"Dad, is the lifeboat coming yet?"

"They'll be here. It won't be long now." He answered with a confidence he didn't possess. Even if the crew found them, the chances of reaching safety from the position they were in was hopeless. Then a thought occurred to him. "How did you call the Coastguard? Do you have my phone?"

Arnie had already checked and knew his phone was missing.

"No," AJ replied sheepishly. "I used my phone."

"Do you still have it?"

"Yes."

"Don't worry, I'm not mad. You've done well so far. Brilliant, really, you have. Does your phone have a flashlight?"

"I don't know, I think so."

"Turn it on. Let's see."

AJ wriggled. Keeping one arm and both legs wrapped around Arnie, he shuffled in his pocket until he produced the handset, an old-fashioned-looking smartphone. He tapped around the front screen until the flashlight came on.

"Good boy," Arnie said. "Now hold it out, facing the sea. Hold it as high as you can, and when the lifeboat arrives, they'll be able to see where we are."

AJ stretched. At that moment a large wave struck, hitting Arnie at waist height and dragging his legs as it subsided. He lost his balance and AJ slipped.

Arnie clung on to him desperately, fighting to maintain his position. The boy cried.

Arnie pushed his back hard against the cliff face. They were okay. Still standing, for now.

"Do you still have the phone?" he asked, holding his boy tight.

"Yes."

Thank you, God.

"Okay, good lad. Don't worry, we're going to be all right. Now hold that phone in the air, as high as you can. Make sure the lifeboat can see us."

Arnie's hope of rescue diminished with every passing second. All he could do was give the boy something to focus on and try to keep them out of the water for as long as possible.

* * * *

The lifeboat heaved mercilessly on the waves. It took all of Dominic's skill at the helm to keep her from capsizing. His old Special Services training had kicked in automatically and he'd managed to put a lid on his personal emotions. He was thinking of nothing but the mission to save the lives of a father and son while keeping his own crew safe.

The sea conditions were among the worst he'd ever known. The only thing they had on their side was daylight, albeit the sky was slate gray and miserable. This near-impossible undertaking would be unfeasible in the dark. To make things worse, the winds hit them side on as they ran parallel to the shore and he had to fight to keep the boat on course.

"*There.* A light," Minty hollered, raising his hand. "Ten o'clock."

Dominic saw nothing but took his crewmate at this word, turning the craft toward the land. His line of sight constantly shifted as the boat rose on the waves and fell into the troughs. "Where?"

"It's gone again," Minty shouted. "Keep going, that way."

As the boat climbed the peak of another wave, Dominic saw the light himself, close to the base of the cliff.

"Shit." They were in a terrible position. The rocks in that location would tear the hull of the boat clean open. He eased nearer, as far as he dared go, keeping clear of the surf and the hidden dangers beneath.

He could just about make out the figures on the rocks. Arnie, supporting his son around his chest. The water was around his thighs. He wouldn't be able to hold on much longer.

"What's the ETA on the helicopter?" he shouted into the radio.

"Eleven minutes," came the reply.

Fuck. They didn't have that long.

He worked the engine, fighting to maintain their position, wondering how the hell he was going to get them out of there.

"We can't go in with the boat," Haig said.

"It'll be too late by the time the helicopter gets here."

Minty was already in the supply box. He produced a long line. "I'll swim in for them. It's the only way. I'll bring them out one at a time. The kid first."

"No," Dominic said. "I'll do it. You keep the boat steady."

"Not a chance," Minty replied. "We need you on the helm. We can't handle the boat the way you do. You know we can't. I'll go in, you keep the boat here till I get back."

Minty was right. It killed Dominic to sit here helplessly while the man he loved and his son were in danger, but he was more use here than in the water. "All right," he shouted. "Do it. Quickly."

He glanced back to the cliff. Arnie and AJ's position looked even more precarious. Dominic struggled to remain calm. He wanted to dive right in and rescue them now, but that was bullshit. He wasn't superman. He could get them all killed. Minty was the man for the job. Dominic had to trust him.

In the next second, all those concerns became irrelevant.

A wave came in and obliterated all sight of Arnie and AJ, and when it retreated the rock where they'd been standing was empty.

The sea had taken them.

* * * *

Paternal instinct overrode everything else. As the wave retreated, Arnie clung tightly to AJ. They were dragged beneath the surface in a furious maelstrom, disorientated as they tumbled over and over. His only concern was to protect the boy. The current pulled them deeper. As he turned over in the water, he saw the gray light of the surface and struck toward it.

The going was tough. Without the use of his arms, and the extra weight, he seemed to make no headway at all. He kicked harder, drawing on every reserve of strength he had, pushing it down into his legs.

His son would not drown in this fucking sea.

At last he broke through. He gasped for air and held AJ up as high as he could.

"Breathe," he shouted, getting a mouthful of salty sea water. The relief he felt when he saw AJ lift his chin and take a deep breath was immense but fleeting. AJ coughed and spluttered.

They were alive, for now.

Arnie looked to the shore. They were about ten yards from the cliff edge. He rolled onto his back and kicked frantically. He had to put some distant between them and the rock. One strong wave was all it would take to smash them to pieces.

Water crashed over their heads, forced them under again.

Arnie gripped AJ even tighter, and the boy clung on.

As soon as he was able, he kicked back to the surface, breaking through and gasping for air again. He rolled onto his back and thrust, desperately trying to get away from the rocks. It became harder with every stroke. Though his arms were locked around AJ, he could no longer feel any sensation in them. Nor his feet. The cold was all-encompassing, stealing over his body, slowing its functions.

AJ's survival was his only concern. Arnie's determination to keep him alive sustained him and kept his limbs moving, kicking through the mercilessly cold water.

Pain was everywhere. In his head, his arms and legs. He fought it.

Keep swimming. Keep moving. Stay alive. Got to stay alive.

The next wave struck, pummeling them deep below the surface, stronger than the ones that preceded it.

When it tore AJ from his grip, there was nothing Arnie could do to stop it.

* * * *

"Where did they go?" Dominic cried.

They'd had a good fix on Arnie and AJ in the water and had been making straight for them when the sea took them under again. He eased back on the throttle. Almost immediately the boat began to roll and pitch in the huge swell. All three men scanned the water, waiting for them to reappear.

Dominic struggled to keep his emotions in check. Things were desperate. Once a casualty entered the water, their chances of survival decreased rapidly. On a day like this, in conditions this bad, there wasn't a second to lose.

Hopelessness threatened to consume him. He fought it back. He wouldn't give in. Not until Arnie and AJ were safe.

"There's the boy," Haig shouted, pointing to port.

Dominic spotted his tiny head, rolling in the swells fifty yards off. He turned the boat quickly, before bringing it carefully up alongside. Haig and Minty reached down, got a hold under each armpit and hauled the tiny figure aboard. From his position at the helm, Dominic saw how bad he looked. Unconscious, cyanosed in the face. The two men lay him on the floor of the boat and checked his vital signs.

"He's alive," Haig called with relief.

He got straight to work administering first aid, while Minty and Dominic resumed the search for Arnie.

Dominic's heart beat hard against his rib cage. He'd never been so personally involved in a rescue.

Come on, honey, where are you? Please don't give up now.

A dark shape appeared on the surface, twenty yards from the boat.

"Starboard," Dominic yelled, turning immediately in that direction.

Minty swapped sides, getting ready as he brought the boat in close.

It was Arnie. Thank God, it was Arnie.

"Gonna need a hand," Minty cried. "He's a big guy."

Dominic kept the boat steady while Minty and Haig leaned over the side. Arnie was unconscious and unable to help himself, dead weight. The men reached beneath his arms and pulled, getting his shoulders above the water before losing their grip and dropping him back in. They grasped again, grabbed him before he disappeared and renewed their effort. As they pulled him a second time, succeeding in getting him clear to the waist, Minty made a grab for his belt. With a secure hold, they were able to haul him up and over the side. They dragged him to the middle of the boat and laid him beside AJ, checking his vital signs.

Please be all right. Come on, Arnie, please don't die. I can't lose you when we've only just met.

"I've got a pulse," Minty shouted. "Get us in."

As the two men got to work, treating Arnie and AJ for the worst of their symptoms, Dominic turned the boat around and raced toward the harbor.

Chapter Twenty

Arnie eventually regained consciousness. A long, slow recovery. He was underwater, at the bottom of the North Sea, nothing above but a ripple of light blue, so far away. *Is this it*? he wondered. *Am I dead?* There were no white lights. No angels. When he tried to swim his limbs were immobile. He was cold one minute and burning up the next. Then he was tumbling from a great height, falling hard and fast before being submerged in the stormy seas again.

At last he opened his eyes. He wasn't lost at the bottom of the ocean. He was in bed, lying on his back, feeling heavy. Movement seemed just as difficult as it had in the dream.

Everything was bright. Florescent strips across the ceiling. White walls.

A figure came closer. A nurse dressed in pale blue.

"Where am I?" he asked. His voice little more than a croak.

"You're in hospital," she answered. "You're safe."

More people came into the room. Doctors. Someone shone a light directly into his eyes. Arnie winced in pain. His thoughts were foggy, painful.

After a few minutes, he drifted off again.

The next time he came around, things were clearer. His head didn't hurt as much. His mind was less muddled.

And sitting at the side of the bed, holding his hand, was Dominic.

Dominic stood up as soon as he realized Arnie was awake. His handsome face was right over him. Arnie could get lost in the warm depths of his eyes.

"Welcome back," Dominic said, his voice soft.

Arnie struggled to smile. He raked through his memories, trying to remember how he'd got here. *The beach, the sea, AJ.*

"Where's AJ?" he asked as his thoughts cleared.

"Don't worry," Dominic said, gripping his hand in reassurance. "He's on his way. He was discharged two days ago. Your parents took him home. When the doctors told me you were coming around, I called them. They'll be here soon."

"Is he all right?"

"He's fine. A little shaken. He's bound to be. He was hypothermic and suffering the effects of shock when we brought him in, but he's good now. More than anything, he's worried about you. We all are."

Arnie relaxed slightly and inhaled. AJ was okay — that was all that mattered.

Dominic put a gentle hand on his brow. Arnie yielded to his touch. He smelled so good, so comforting and familiar.

"It's such a relief to see you awake," Dominic said. "I was worried we were going to lose you."

"Did you find us? Were you in the lifeboat?"

"I was. I wouldn't have stopped searching until I found you. You're everything to me now. I couldn't bear to lose you."

"What happened?" Arnie asked, digging deeper into this mind. "Someone hit me from behind."

"Don't worry about that now. It's not important."

"Tell me," he insisted. "I want to know."

"Is that all you remember? Being taken from behind?"

He nodded.

"Noel Garrard. The kid who helps at the station. He's the one who attacked you. He must have followed you and AJ along the beach. He knocked you out cold and left you to the mercy of the incoming tide. If AJ hadn't reacted the way he did and dragged you onto the higher rocks before calling for help, you wouldn't be here now."

"But why? I don't understand. Why did he clobber me?"

"We can go over this later," Dominic said, stroking his hair.

"I want to know now."

Dominic sat and pulled the chair closer to the bed. "The police suspect Noel is the man who threw Sandy Costello over the cliff. I don't know much yet. The investigators are keeping the facts down tight, but they found evidence at his house that proves he did it. They also suspect he's been hanging round your house these last two weeks. Your stalker, that was him."

"Why?"

"Why did he attack Sandy? I have no idea. I suspect the reason he focused on you is that you and AJ saw what he did. You couldn't ID him, but I don't know, I guess he panicked in case you could. Or he became fixated on you because you had a connection to his first crime. Until the police catch up with him, we'll never know."

"What do you mean, catch up with him?"

"He's gone to ground. No one has seen him since Saturday."

Arnie stiffened. Dominic took his hand again.

"Don't worry," he continued. "There's a police officer stationed right outside that door. And another at your parents' house watching over AJ. They'll be with you until they apprehend him. You're both safe. And I won't let the little bastard anywhere near you. He should hope the cops catch up with him before I do, because I won't be responsible for my actions."

"This is crazy," Arnie said. "Why the hell would he do any of this?"

"Noel Garrard is a disturbed young man. He always has been. His grandmother asked us to get him involved with the lifeboat in the hope it would give him something positive to focus on. That the crew could act as role models to him. His parents were worse than useless. His dad went to jail for armed robbery when Noel was just a kid and died a couple of years later. A feud or something with another inmate that got out of hand. His mother was a heroin addict with a string of abusive boyfriends. Noel was removed from her care and placed with his grandparents when he was ten. Your mother will be able to tell the story better than I can, but the grandparents have done their best for him. They made him go to school and tried to give him a normal life to stop him turning out like his mother and father."

"None of that explains what he did."

"No," Dominic said carefully. "Honey, there's worse. I just don't think now is the time."

Arnie gripped his hand. "Tell me."

"You've just woken up."

"Tell me," Arnie insisted.

Dominic took a breath before looking him straight in the eye. "Gabriel is dead. They found him at home on Saturday afternoon, not long before you were attacked. The police want Noel for that too."

"*Dead?*" Arnie heard the words. He understood their meaning. He could not believe them. "How?"

"They think it happened sometime on Friday night. All indications are that he was taken by surprise when he got home from work. When he didn't come in the next day, someone from the restaurant went looking for him."

Tears sprang under Arnie's eyelids and ran down his cheeks. "Why? For fuck's sake, why?"

"Until they catch Noel, we'll never know. Maybe we never will. I can't imagine what provoked him to do any of this. He was a quiet kid, sullen most of the time, and motivating him to do anything around the station was a chore in itself. But he showed no inclination toward violence. I can't remember hearing him swear or speak out of turn. On the surface of things, he seemed rather placid, docile even. There must have been some deep, dangerous currents running beneath that calm exterior."

Arnie wiped his eyes on the back of his hand. "I can't believe Gabriel is dead. What did he do to him?"

Dominic shook his head. "You don't need to know about that yet. I'll tell you everything later, when you're ready. I promise. For now, I want you to focus on getting better. You were in a bad way, you know. Concussion, hypothermia and shock. You've got a couple of broken ribs too. Your body was shutting down when we got you to the dock."

"I'll mend," he said resolutely.

Dominic smiled. "That's right. You will. You're a fighter and a survivor. You and AJ, you boys are made of strong stuff."

"What about Sandy Costello? I got a news alert, right before Noel hit me. It said she had come around."

"That's right, she has. She's going to be all right too. Eventually. The poor girl has a lot of broken bones, including her pelvis. Fortunately, there's no damage to her skull or spinal column. She's got a long road ahead of her and a lot of intensive physio before she'll be fully healed, but she's on her way. It's a miracle, really, considering what she has been through. She's a fighter, like you."

Arnie nodded, then sighed. "What could drive a young man to do these terrible things? I don't buy the useless parents as an excuse. Plenty of kids come from bad backgrounds. It doesn't turn them into callous killers. There must be some reason."

"We might never know. Don't torture yourself trying to figure it out. Noel is disturbed. No one could have predicted he'd do any of these things. Whatever is wrong with him, he kept it well hidden. It's hard, I know, but you must focus on the positives here. Your son is alive. *You* are alive. They'll catch up with Noel soon enough. I doubt he's got the brains to evade the police for too long."

Arnie nodded and wiped his eyes again. "You saved us."

"It was AJ. If he wasn't smart enough to do what he did and call the Coastguard, we wouldn't have been there. Your boy is a hero."

Arnie took his hand. "Then I guess I really am lucky. To have two heroes in my life."

Epilogue

One year later

Saturday. A glorious afternoon in early August. The patio and lawn of Cliff House were thronged with people in short-sleeved shirts and summer dresses. At the bottom of the garden, a professional caterer served up barbequed meat and fish, with a wide selection of salads and fruits. Closer to the house, in the shade of a gazebo, two barmen kept the guests fulfilled with an endless supply of beer, wine and Pimm's.

From the cool interior of the kitchen, through the open French doors, Arnie watched those closest and most loved to him enjoying themselves in the sun. AJ played with his cousins with complete abandon. The move north had done wonders for the boy. Arnie had never seen him so happy, or as boisterous as he was these days. Following their release from hospital a year ago, Arnie had expected AJ would want to return to London as soon as possible. That he'd never want to be near water again. Against expectations, the opposite was true. Instead of running away from North Point, he didn't want to leave.

'*Can we stay, Dad?*' he'd asked, the day after they discharged Arnie. '*Please.*'

AJ had been insistent. They had connections here, family. They were loved and supported in ways they couldn't be down south. Arnie was almost as surprised when he agreed. Despite everything that had happened, this *was* their home. London was a place of work, somewhere for AJ to go to school. But it had never been home. That was Nyemouth.

The police had caught up with Noel Garrard a week after he went on the run. He'd made it as far south as Nottingham, begging, stealing, hitchhiking. His goal, he'd later said, was to reach Dover and steal away on the back of a lorry to the continent. He'd been apprehended at a bus station, when a ticket agent had recognized him from the news. He had not resisted arrest, and when he'd appeared before the magistrates the following day, his case had been committed to Crown Court and the bench had remanded him into custody.

Many theories regarding his motives had been debated, but when he was next in court, Noel had entered a guilty plea to one count of Murder and three counts of Attempted Murder, negating the necessity of a trial. The judge had requested a pre-sentence report, together with a separate psychiatric report. Neither had produced any answers. Noel had been uncooperative and refused to offer any reason for his acts of violence.

In a victim impact statement, Sandy Costello attested that she had never met Noel Garrard until their encounter on North Point. It appeared she had been selected entirely at random. It could have been anyone he chose to lash out at. Sandy had the misfortune of being in the wrong place at the wrong time.

The press speculated that Noel targeted Arnie and AJ because they were the only witnesses to what he'd done. It seemed the most likely explanation, but with Noel's refusal to confirm it, they would never be sure. They could only guess at his reason for killing Gabriel. The obvious link was Arnie. Whether he'd killed Gabriel to hurt Arnie or had some warped plan of framing him for the crime remained a mystery.

Noel had been sentenced to life imprisonment with a minimum tariff of twenty-five years. He wouldn't be eligible for parole until he was forty-four. AJ would be in his early thirties when the time came. Despite his best efforts not to dwell on it, the implication of what might happen when that day came around kept Arnie awake some nights.

For now, AJ was doing fine. That was what he had to focus on.

Earlier in the year, AJ had been given a Children of Courage Award for Outstanding Bravery at a ceremony in Manchester. Arnie owed his life to the incredible actions of his son. He would make certain they were never in a situation like that again.

Watching him now, Arnie smiled. AJ sat in the garden at a table with his cousins and a handful of new friends he'd made here in the town. They were eating bowls of trifle and had cream and custard smeared across their faces and the table. They were kids. Happy and carefree. Exactly as they should be.

There were so many people out there who meant the world to Arnie. His parents, his sister, even her husband, Cyrus. The man was a pain in the arse, but he was family. The lifeboat crew were here too, together with their own families.

And Sandy Costello with her boyfriend, Jamie.

She looked lovely in a white-and-red pattern sundress. A year on, the results of her accident were barely noticeable. She walked with an uneven gait and was troubled with back pain but had made a remarkable recovery. Since getting out of hospital, she and Arnie had become good friends. She'd met Jamie, a former soldier who had lost his left leg to a landmine, at one of her rehabilitation sessions. They got on well and seemed to make each other happy. Arnie was thrilled for her.

Gazing out of the doors, lost in contemplation, he snapped out of it as Dominic walked through the frame.

"Why are you hiding away in here?" Dominic asked with a dazzling grin. "This is your housewarming party."

After making the decision to return to Nyemouth, Arnie had contacted the owners of Cliff House and made them an offer to buy the place. The final completion had gone through a month ago.

"I just needed a few minutes out of the sun," he said. "It's hot out there."

"Oh yeah," Dominic said, coming in for a kiss. "It's pretty hot in here too." He gave Arnie's arse a cheeky squeeze.

Dominic. Probably the biggest reason to stay in North Point. Their love for each other deepened every day.

For the last three months they'd even been working together, collaborating on a book. Though he'd always been a deeply private person, Arnie had accepted a commission from a publisher to write a book about his experiences. Arnie told the story and Dominic, the experienced writer, put it down on paper. It had been an intense, cathartic experience, and they were almost done. Once complete, they'd agreed the royalties from the book would be split three ways—one third would go to Gabriel's family, a third to Sandy and a third to the lifeboat service.

They kissed long and deep.

Now that the deal on Cliff House had been finalized, Dominic had agreed to move in with Arnie and AJ and would put his own house up for rental.

"I think we should go back outside before we get carried away," Arnie said, sliding his palm across Dominic's butt.

Dominic kissed him back. "Agreed. Let's enjoy this with the people we love. We'll have plenty of time for each other later."

Arnie couldn't agree more.

With their arms around each other, they walked out into the sun. United and completely in love.

Want to see more from this author? Here's a taster for you to enjoy!

Anthem: Anthem of the Sea
Thom Collins

Excerpt

The taxi collected Daniel Blake from the hotel on time. He liked that. Punctuality, efficiency and professionalism — three things he valued in all areas of his career. Be on time and be prepared — that had been his motto since he was fourteen years old. Fifteen years later, he continued to live by it.

He helped the driver load his gear into the trunk. There wasn't much of it. When on the road, he traveled light with just a medium-sized case, a holdall and a suit carrier. He'd arrived in Lisbon the previous morning, disembarking from a cruise ship, where he'd performed for two nights. His shirts would need washing and his suit pressing before his next show. There was plenty of time.

He gave the driver directions to his designated cruise terminal and climbed onto the back seat. Thankfully, the air conditioning was running. Though it was late October, the outside temperature remained in the mid-eighties and it wasn't even eleven o'clock. Last night he had heard some of the hotel staff complain about the weather turning cold, but for a boy like him, born and raised in the northeast of England, these climates were well above average. Back home, this would be a hot day in June or July.

It was a short drive to the port. Early in the day, but the streets were busy. Three massive cruise ships were anchored in the harbor, discharging thousands of eager tourists into the city. British, American, German, Japanese, they scurried through the streets, clutching backpacks and maps, keen to explore as much as they could of the historic Portuguese city in the few hours they had here.

Daniel smiled at their faces as they zipped by.

Lisbon, his last stop before home.

The car arrived at the port and within ten minutes Daniel stood beside the gangway with his luggage, waiting for the necessary security calls to be made that would allow him to board the ship. The enormous vessel towered above him, casting a huge shadow across the dock. The *Atlantic* was one of the biggest and most spectacular cruise ships in the world.

There were a lot of criticisms for super ships such as this. He'd heard them described as floating shopping malls, grotesque monstrosities and budget hotels at sea, but for Daniel there was something quite majestic about the craft and its design, to say nothing of the engineering that went into the construction of such a huge vessel.

"Those things are so top heavy," a jobbing magician once had told him in a bar. "I hear they roll right over in high seas."

Daniel had laughed at the man's ignorance. "And when did you last hear of that happening?"

The man had floundered. "I'm just saying that something so uneven can't be safe, can it? You won't ever catch me on one of them things. Mug's game, isn't it?"

"It's your loss," Daniel had told him cheerily. He felt safer at sea, even in the roughest weather, than he ever had on a plane. Motorways too. It might not be the quickest, but without a doubt it was the most luxurious and extravagant way to travel. He loved being at sea.

Waiting for the security guy to return with his passport, Daniel realized he'd drawn some attention.

A slow stream of passengers was returning to the ship. They couldn't have seen much of Lisbon, coming back already. Among them was an English family. While the parents lit cigarettes before joining the embarkation queue, the daughter, who looked around fourteen, stared directly at him.

"Hi." He smiled. "Good day out?"

The girl was plump and pretty with wavy brown hair that fell around her shoulders. She wore a sweet, flowery sundress and red Converse shoes. She blushed as she realized she'd been caught gawking.

"Are you...? Oh, my God, you are, aren't you? You're Daniel Blake."

He raised his hands in mock surrender. "Guilty as charged. Don't shoot me."

The girl nervously stepped forward, looking at him with wide, hazel eyes. "What are you doing here?"

"I'm waiting to join the ship. I'm performing on board."

Her jaw fell. "The *Anthem?* You're coming on the *Anthem?*"

He nodded. He didn't mind being recognized like this. Daniel was famous enough in the UK, but not so much that it ever became an inconvenience. His fame came from a TV talent show. The public had made him and he appreciated all the support he got.

"Oh my God." The girl's face became highly animated. "*Mam! Dad!* Come here. Oh my God, you won't believe it. *Daniel Blake.* It's actually him."

Her bemused parents stubbed out their cigarettes and came over. They were an attractive-looking couple of around forty. The girl looked a lot like her father.

"I hope she's not bothering you," the dad said, looking cautiously between Daniel and his daughter.

"Not a bit," Daniel assured him. "It's a pleasure."

"Daniel is going to be singing on the ship. Can you believe it? How cool is that?" She grinned a mile wide.

"Starting tomorrow," he said. "Make certain you get yourselves a great seat down front. I can use all the support I can get."

"I will, I will. I voted for you every week on *The One.* You were my favorite from the start."

"So it's you I need to thank for winning. What's your name, sweetie?"

"Julieann."

"Well, thank you, Julieann. Your votes changed my life."

The girl blushed violently.

The security officer came back to escort Daniel onto the ship. Before boarding, he posed for photographs with Julieann and her family.

"The girls at school will have a fit when they see these on Instagram," Julieann said proudly as they took a selfie together.

"See you at the shows," Daniel said as he walked on board. "And don't forget—front row. Be there. I'll look out for you."

"We'll definitely be there."

Once on board, he passed his luggage through the security scanner and was equipped with his sea pass ID, the plastic card that would enable him to move around the ship, access his accommodation and run a tab in the bars and shops. He was greeted on the far side of security by a young woman in a blue shirt and khaki shorts. Her soft blonde hair was tied back from her round, attractive face. She was vaguely familiar from his engagement earlier in the season. He checked her name badge to refresh his memory. Belle Hodges, entertainment crew, from South Australia.

"Hi," Belle said cheerily. "It's wonderful to have you back on board."

She extended her hand and he shook it. "It's great to be back. Honestly, I've been looking forward to this since I left in May. How has your maiden season gone?"

"Over too quickly and totally ace. I can't believe it's been that long since you were here. Yikes, the time has flown. Let me give you a hand with your stuff."

"That's okay. I can manage. Just point me in the right direction and I'll find my way."

Ignoring his protests, Belle took up the suit carrier.

"You're in real luck," she said. "You've been allocated a large stateroom on one of the passenger decks. Balcony and all."

"You're joking? Wow. Am I sharing with the house band or a football team?"

Belle giggled, wrinkling her nose. "Silly. You've got the whole place to yourself."

"Seriously? What gives? I never get accommodation like that."

Belle looked around cautiously and lowered her voice. "We had a family thrown off the ship in Gran Canaria so you've got their room. They caused a fight in the martini bar and punched an officer who tried to intervene. Captain Rassimov put them off at the next port. No second chances."

"Good to know we're in such firm hands."

"Captain Rassimov is the best," Belle gushed.

Daniel didn't doubt it. He'd met the dashing captain on his last trip. Tall, dark, handsome and extremely charismatic, he sent hearts beating fast among the passengers and crew. If he wasn't so straight, Daniel would fancy him too. Rassimov was the perfect man to master such a grand vessel.

Launched in May, with a rumored cost of over one-point-five billion, the *Atlantic Anthem* was coming to the end of its inaugural European season. It was the newest and biggest vessel in the Royal Atlantic fleet. Daniel had spent two nights on board when he'd performed a headline set on the maiden voyage. He'd worked for cruise companies all over the world, but he couldn't fail to be impressed by the *Anthem*. It was billed as the ship with everything. From his own experience that was certainly true.

As he walked through the decks with Belle, his sense of excitement increased. The interior was truly splendid. Not a penny had been spared, from the lush carpets to the paintings and sculptures that graced every deck. Before coming on board, he'd read all the specs — about the spa and fitness center, two swimming pools and a solarium, the Royal Theater with nine-hundred-sixty seats, the bars — eight of them across the ship — the main dining room plus three specialty restaurants and a twenty-four-hour café. Several public entertainment areas were situated on Decks Four and Five around a jaw-dropping central staircase. Knowing all of that in advance, he still had been blown away when he'd came upon the ship for the first time. And he felt it now, all over again.

Only the most jaded, spoiled and hard-to-please traveler could fail to be inspired by the *Anthem*.

They rode one of the glass elevators to the tenth floor where Belle led him down a long corridor to his stateroom in the forward section of the ship.

"Last time, I had an interior cabin in the crew quarters." He laughed.

"Yep, that's where they like to cram us in. But now you've got this."

Daniel swiped his sea pass card to enter the room. A major step up from crew class, the room was bright and contemporary, to the standard of any good hotel. He had an enormous double bed all to himself and a sitting area with a long, cream leather sofa. There was a dressing table, minibar, TV, private bathroom and balcony.

"I hope I don't get lost in here," he joked, dumping his luggage by the wardrobe.

"As long as you're on stage for your shows tomorrow night, no one will mind what you get up to in here," Belle said.

"You can put your mind at ease on that count," he said. "I've been performing since I was fourteen and I've never missed a show in my life."

Belle left him to settle in. Daniel unpacked his clothes first and filled a plastic bag with stuff that needed washing immediately—shirts, socks and underwear. Another great thing about working on a luxury cruise liner—everything was to hand. If he left the bag out today, all the items would be washed, ironed and returned by tomorrow.

He went into the bathroom next, laying out his razor, toothbrush and skincare products. He brought everything with him when he traveled. Though he wasn't particularly vain, it was important to look good in public.

He didn't have to worry. At twenty-nine years old — five months shy of thirty — he was in prime condition. He'd never looked better. For years he used to hate the way he looked. Everything about him had been out of proportion, especially his face. Eyes, teeth, nose, chin, they were always too big. But throughout his twenties, the rest of his body had caught up. He'd filled out and gained muscle and his face, which had seemed so awkward in his teens, had developed an extraordinary handsomeness. He had a strong jaw with a cowboy cleft, while his mouth was wide and masculine. With sky-blue eyes and thick brown hair, he had become a good-looking man. Very good-looking.

His confidence hadn't grown to match his looks. A part of him would always be that skinny, peculiar kid. But only he could see it.

Finally unpacked, he relaxed and walked onto the balcony. He had a great view of the city and the people below, streaming like ants around the port terminals. Daniel took a moment to enjoy it all. He loved just about every part of the cruise experience.

Every ship, every voyage, was a new adventure.

The *Atlantic Anthem* promised a greater adventure than any other.

He couldn't wait to get started.

PUBLISHING

Sign up for our newsletter and find out about all our romance book releases, eBook sales and promotions, sneak peeks and FREE romance books!

About the Author

Thom Collins is the author of Closer by Morning, with Pride Publishing. His love of page turning thrillers began at an early age when his mother caught him reading the latest Jackie Collins book and promptly confiscated it, sparking a life-long love of raunchy novels.

Thom has lived in the North East of England his whole life. He grew up in Northumberland and now lives in County Durham with his husband and two cats. He loves all kinds of genre fiction, especially bonkbusters, thrillers, romance and horror. He is also a cookery book addict with far too many titles cluttering his shelves. When not writing he can be found in the kitchen trying out new recipes. He's a keen traveler but with a fear of flying that gets worse with age, but since taking his first cruise in 2013 he realized that sailing is the way to go.

Thom loves to hear from readers. You can find his contact information, website details and author profile page at https://www.pride-publishing.com